ISLAND BOYZ

other books by
graham salisbury

Lord of the Deep

Jungle Dogs

Shark Bait

Under the Blood-Red Sun

Blue Skin of the Sea

ISLAND BOYZ

short stories

graham salisbury

WENDY
LAMB
BOOKS

Published by
Wendy Lamb Books
an imprint of
Random House Children's Books
a division of Random House, Inc.
1540 Broadway
New York, New York 10036

Visit us on the Web! www.randomhouse.com/teens
Educators and librarians, for a variety of teaching tools, visit us at
www.randomhouse.com/teachers

Library of Congress Cataloging-in-Publication Data

Salisbury, Graham.
Island boyz / Graham Salisbury.
p. cm.
Contents: Island boyz—The ravine—Mrs. Noonan—Forty bucks—
The hurricane—Aumakua—Frankie Diamond is robbing us blind—
Waiting for the war—Doi store monkey—Angel baby—Hat of clouds.
ISBN 0-385-90037-6 (lib. bdg.)—ISBN 0-385-72970-7
1. Hawaii—Juvenile fiction. [1. Hawaii—Fiction. 2. Short stories.]
I. Title.

PZ7.S15225 Is 2002
[Fic]—dc21

2001032425

The text of this book is set in 12-point Garamond.

Book design by Patrice Sheridan

Manufactured in the United States of America

April 2002

10 9 8 7 6 5 4 3 2 1

BVG

For all the guys I kicked around with
in Kaneohe, Kailua, Honolulu,
Kailua-Kona, Hilo, and Kamuela.
You inspire me still.

Bobby, Terry, Roger, Freddie, Dale,
Dickie, Dougie, Mark, Gordie, Kenny, Mike,
Charlie, Junior, David, Guy, Johnny, Keoki,
Wayne, Spooks, Ata, Kit, Tommy, Curtis, Barry,
Monty, Larry, Pini, James, Jamie, Jim, Jimmy,
Sam, Ipo, Reggie, Robin, I.J., Gene, Robster,
Vic, Ernie, Peter, Frank, Leland, Henry, Steve,
George, Jerome, Robby, Tuck, Mel, Curt,
Frosty, Tioni, Chuckie, Chris, Bill, Willy,
DoveBeak, Koki, and Keo.

Island boyz.
Lucky us.

contents

Island Boyz

we wore rubber slippers
and boroboro clothes
biked to the beach with
boards under our arms
surfed our brains out
hour after hour after hour
got out with useless rubbery arms
stole papayas
right off somebody's tree
broke them open
savaged them into our mouths
hoping to calm our raging hunger

nothing could beat
papayas after the ocean

sometimes we bounced down
dusty back roads in
the bed of somebody's

beat-up old pickup
joking and laughing or saying nothing
sitting back there on old tires
and crushed cardboard boxes
sometimes telling stupid jokes
or bragging about
whatever we could dredge up
or make up
nodding to the thumping
radio in the cab

and then when the sun
lay low on the sea
we wandered down
to the harbor
to drink from
corroded spigots on the pier
icy clear water
tangy like iron
swiping our dripping chins
on the shoulder of our T-shirts and
watching the fishing boats
crawl home with fish flags flying
deckhands standing cool
on the bow with rope in their hands
man-oh-man did I dream
of one day
standing like that
so cool
so important

often just after
the green flash of sunset
we spread out on the rocks
at the edge of the sea
with guitars and baritone ukes
and cold sweaty-canned drinks
talking low
feeling tall
dreaming of girls
of love
and nothing could possibly
have touched that

in the starry black night
we sat under palm trees
talking story
getting dizzy on punchy laughter
probably looking to anyone
who might have seen us
like some weird tribe
of little half men
poi dogs
haole
hawaiian
japanese
chinese
filipino
portuguese
korean
tongan

samoan
whatever
a strange brew mixed by sun
salt and seawater
idiots and geniuses
friends who stood by you
no matter what
yeah

   and if luck paid us a visit
we lingered long on the beach
deep into the night
with girls we didn't deserve
girls who smelled like plumerias
and spoke in whispers
that tickled our ears
whose soft cheeks
sent us reeling
and that was best of all
the girls
on the beach
at night

   we drifted home late
one by one
waving
nodding
tomorrow brah
to houses ruled by
cock-a-roaches
centipedes

cane spiders
fat black flies
mosquitoes
and crawled blissfully into bed
to sleep like stones
hardly noticing the bugs
and anyway who cared
not us
no never us

island boyz
not boys
boyz

I would not have
traded places
with anyone
not even
God

The Ravine

When Vinny and three others dropped down into the ravine, they entered a jungle thick with tangled trees and rumors of what might have happened to the dead boy's body.

The muddy trail was slick and dangerous, especially in places where it had fallen away. The cool breeze that swept the Hawaiian hillside pastures above died early in the descent.

There were four of them—Vinny; his best friend, Joe-Boy; Mo who was afraid of nothing, and Joe-Boy's haole girlfriend, Starlene, all fifteen. It was a Tuesday in July, two weeks and a day after the boy had drowned. If, in fact, that's what had happened to him.

Vinny slipped, and dropped his towel in the mud. He picked it up and tried to brush it off, but instead smeared the mudspot around until the towel looked like something his dog had slept on. "Tst," he said.

Joe-Boy, hiking down just behind him, laughed.

"Hey, Vinny, just think, that kid walked where you walking."

"Shuddup," Vinny said.

"You prob'ly stepping right where his foot was."

Vinny moved to the edge of the trail where the ravine fell through a twisted jungle of gnarly trees and underbrush to the stream far below.

Joe-Boy laughed again. "You such a queen, Vinny. You know that?"

Vinny could see Starlene and Mo farther ahead, their heads bobbing as they walked, both almost down to the pond where the boy had died.

"Hey," Joe-Boy went on, "maybe you going be the one to find his body."

"You don't cut it out, Joe-Boy, I going . . . I going . . ."

"What? Cry?"

Vinny scowled. Sometimes Joe-Boy was a big fat babooze.

They slid down the trail. Mud oozed between Vinny's toes. He grabbed at roots and branches to keep from falling. Mo and Starlene were out of sight now, the trail ahead having cut back.

Joe-Boy said, "You going jump in the water and go down and your hand going touch his face, stuck under the rocks. *Hahaha . . . ahahaha!*"

Vinny winced. He didn't want to be here. It was too soon, way too soon. Two weeks and one day.

He saw a footprint in the mud and stepped around it.

The dead boy had jumped and had never come back up. Four search-and-rescue divers hunted for two days straight and never found him. Gave Vinny the creeps. It didn't make sense. The pond wasn't that big.

He wondered why it didn't seem to bother anyone else. Maybe it did, and they just didn't want to say.

Butchie was the kid's name. Only fourteen.

Fourteen.

Two weeks and one day ago he was walking down this trail. Now, nobody could find him.

The jungle crushed in, reaching over the trail, and Vinny brushed leafy branches aside. The roar of the waterfall got louder, louder.

Starlene said it was the goddess that took him, the one that lives in the stone down by the road. She did that every now and then, Starlene said, took somebody when she got lonely. Took him and kept him. Vinny had heard that legend before, but he'd never believed in it.

Now he didn't know what he believed.

The body had to be stuck down there. But still, four divers and they couldn't find it?

Vinny decided he'd better believe in the legend.

If he didn't, the goddess might get mad and send him bad luck. Or maybe take *him,* too.

Stopstopstop! Don't think like that.

"Come on," Joe-Boy said, nudging Vinny from behind. "Hurry it up."

Just then, Starlene whooped, her voice bouncing around the walls of the ravine.

"Let's *go*," Joe-Boy said. "They there already."

Moments later Vinny jumped up onto a large boulder at the edge of the pond. Starlene was swimming out in the brown water. It wasn't murky brown but clean and clear to a depth of maybe three or four feet. Because of the waterfall you had to yell if you wanted to say something. The whole place smelled of mud and ginger and iron.

Starlene swam across to the waterfall on the far side of the pond and ducked under it, then climbed out and edged along the rock wall behind it, moving slowly, like a spider. Above, sun-sparkling stream water spilled over the lip of a one-hundred-foot drop.

Mo and Joe-Boy threw their towels onto the rocks and dove into the pond. Vinny watched, his muddy towel hooked around his neck. Reluctantly he let it fall, then dove in after them.

The cold mountain water tasted tangy. Was it because the boy's body was down there decomposing? He spat it out.

He followed Joe-Boy and Mo to the waterfall and ducked under it. They climbed up onto the

rock ledge, just as Starlene had done, then spi-
dered their way over to where you could climb to
a small ledge about fifteen feet up. They took their
time, because the hand- and footholds were slimy
with moss.

Starlene jumped first. Her shriek echoed off the
rocky cliff, then died in the dense green jungle.

Mo jumped, then Joe-Boy, then Vinny.

The fifteen-foot ledge was not the problem.

It was the one above it, the one you had to
work up to, the big one, where you had to take a
deadly zigzag trail that climbed up and away from
the waterfall, then cut back and forth to a foot-
wide ledge something more like fifty feet up.

That was the problem.

That was where the boy had jumped from.

Joe-Boy and Starlene swam out to the middle
of the pond. Mo swam back under the waterfall
and climbed once again to the fifteen-foot ledge.

Vinny started to swim out toward Joe-Boy but
stopped when he saw Starlene put her arms
around him. She kissed him. They sank under for a
long time, then came back up, still kissing.

Joe-Boy saw Vinny looking and winked. "You
like that, Vinny? Watch, I show you how." He
kissed Starlene again.

Vinny turned away and swam back over to the
other side of the pond, where he'd first gotten in.
His mother would kill him if she ever heard about
where he'd come. After the boy drowned, or was
taken by the goddess, or whatever happened to

him, she said never to come to this pond again. Ever. It was off-limits. Permanently.

But not his dad. He said, "You fall off a horse, you get back on, right? Or else you going be scared of it all your life."

His mother scoffed and waved him off. "Don't listen to him, Vinny, listen to me. Don't go there. That pond is haunted." Which had made his dad laugh.

But Vinny promised he'd stay away.

But then Starlene and Joe-Boy said, "Come with us anyway. You let your mommy run your life, or what?" And Vinny said, "But what if I get caught?" And Joe-Boy said, "So?"

Vinny mashed his lips. He was so weak. Couldn't even say no. But if he'd said, "I can't go, my mother won't like it," they would have laughed him right off the island. He had to go. No choice.

So far it was fine. He'd even gone in the water. Everyone was happy. All he had to do now was wait it out and go home and hope his mother never heard about it.

When he looked up, Starlene was gone.

He glanced around the pond until he spotted her starting up the zigzag trail to the fifty-foot ledge. She was moving slowly, hanging on to roots and branches on the upside of the cliff. He couldn't believe she was going there. He wanted to yell, "Hey, Starlene, that's where he *died*!"

But she already knew that.

Mo jumped from the lower ledge, yelling

"Banzaiiii!" An explosion of coffee-colored water erupted when he hit.

Joe-Boy swam over to where Starlene had gotten out. He waved to Vinny, grinning like a fool, then followed Starlene up the zigzag trail.

Now Starlene was twenty-five, thirty feet up. Vinny watched her for a while, then lost sight of her when she slipped behind a wall of jungle that blocked his view. A few minutes later she popped back out, now almost at the top where the trail ended, where there was nothing but mud and a few plants to grab on to if you slipped, plants that would rip right out of the ground, plants that wouldn't stop you if you fell, nothing but your screams between you and the rocks below.

Just watching her, Vinny felt his stomach tingle. He couldn't imagine what it must feel like to be up there, especially if you were afraid of heights, like he was. She has no fear, Vinny thought, no fear at all. Pleasepleaseplease, Starlene. I don't want to see you die.

Starlene crept forward, making her way to the end of the trail where the small ledge was.

Joe-Boy popped out of the jungle behind her. He stopped, waiting for her to jump before going on.

Vinny held his breath.

Starlene, in her cutoff jeans and soaked T-shirt, stood perfectly still, her arms at her side. Vinny suddenly felt like hugging her. Why, he couldn't tell. Starlene, please.

She reached behind her and took a wide leaf from a plant, then eased down and scooped up a finger of mud. She made a brown cross on her forehead, then wiped her muddy fingers on her jeans.

She waited.

Was she thinking about the dead boy?

She stuck the stem end of the leaf in her mouth, leaving the rest of it to hang out. When she jumped, the leaf would flap up and cover her nose and keep water from rushing into it. An old island trick.

She jumped.

Down, down.

Almost in slow motion, it seemed at first, then faster and faster. She fell feet first, arms flapping to keep balance so she wouldn't land on her back or stomach, which would probably almost kill her.

Just before she hit, she crossed her arms over her chest and vanished within a small explosion of rusty water.

Vinny stood, not breathing at all, praying.

Ten seconds. Twenty, thirty . . .

She came back up, laughing.

She shouldn't make fun that way, Vinny thought. It was asking for it.

Vinny looked up when he heard Joe-Boy shout, "Hey, Vinny, watch how a man does it! Look!"

Joe-Boy scooped up some mud and made a bolt of lightning across his chest. When he jumped, he threw himself out, face and body parallel to the pond, his arms and legs spread out. He's *crazy,* Vinny thought, absolutely insane. At the last second, Joe-Boy folded into a ball and hit. *Ca-roomp!* He came up whooping and yelling, "*Wooo!* So *good*! Come on, Vinny, it's hot!"

Vinny faked a laugh. He waved, shouting, "Nah, the water's too cold!"

Now Mo was heading up the zigzag trail, Mo who hardly ever said a word and would do anything anyone ever challenged him to do. Come on, Mo, not you, too. Vinny knew then that he would have to jump.

Jump, or never live it down.

Mo jumped in the same way Joe-Boy had, man-style, splayed out in a suicide fall. He came up grinning.

Starlene and Joe-Boy turned toward Vinny.

Vinny got up and hiked around the edge of the pond, walking in the muddy shallows, looking at a school of small brown-back fish near a ginger patch.

Maybe they'd forget about him.

Starlene torpedoed over, swimming under water. Her body glittered in the small amount of sunlight that penetrated the trees around the rim of the ravine. When she came up, she broke the surface smoothly, gracefully, like a swan. Her blond hair sleeked back like river grass.

She smiled a sweet smile. "Joe-Boy says you're afraid to jump. I didn't believe him. He's wrong, right?"

Vinny said quickly, "Of course he's wrong. I just don't want to, that's all. The water's cold."

"Nah, it's nice."

Vinny looked away. On the other side of the pond Joe-Boy and Mo were on the cliff behind the waterfall.

"Joe-Boy says your mom told you not to come here. Is that true?"

Vinny nodded. "Yeah. Stupid, but she thinks it's haunted."

"She's right."

"What?"

"That boy didn't die, Vinny. The stone goddess took him. He's in a good place right now. He's her prince."

Vinny scowled. He couldn't tell if Starlene was teasing him or if she really believed that. He said, "Yeah, prob'ly."

"Are you going to jump, or is Joe-Boy right?"

"Joe-Boy's an idiot. Sure I'm going to jump."

Starlene grinned, staring at Vinny a little too long. "He is an idiot, isn't he? But I love him."

"Yeah, well . . ."

"Go to it, big boy. I'll be watching."

Starlene sank down and swam out into the pond.

Ca-ripes.

Vinny ripped a hank of white ginger from the ginger patch and smelled it and prayed he'd still be alive after the sun went down.

He took his time climbing the zigzag trail.

When he got to the part where the jungle hid him from view, he stopped and smelled the ginger again. So sweet and alive it made Vinny wish for all he was worth that he were climbing out of the ravine right now, heading home.

But of course, there was no way he could do that.

Not before jumping.

He tossed the ginger onto the muddy trail and continued on. He slipped once or twice, maybe three times. He didn't keep track. He was too numb now, too caught up in the insane thing he was about to do. He'd never been this far up the trail before. Once, he'd tried to go all the way but couldn't. It made him dizzy.

When he stepped out and the jungle opened into a huge bowl where he could look down, way, way down, he could see there three heads in the water, heads with arms moving slowly to keep them afloat, and a few bright rays of sunlight pouring down onto them, and when he saw this his stomach fluttered and rose. Something sour came up and he spat it out.

It made him wobble to look down. He closed his eyes. His whole body trembled. The trail was no wider than the length of his foot. And it was wet and muddy from little rivulets of water that bled from the side of the cliff.

The next few steps were the hardest he'd ever taken in his life. He tried not to look down, but he couldn't help it. His gaze was drawn there. He struggled to push back an urge to fly, just jump off and fly. He could almost see himself spiraling down like a glider, or a bird, or a leaf.

His hands shook as if he were freezing. He wondered: Had the dead boy felt this way? Or had he felt brave, like Starlene or Joe-Boy, or Mo, who seemed to feel nothing?

Somebody shouted from below, but Vinny couldn't make it out over the waterfall roaring down just feet beyond the ledge where he would soon be standing, cascading past so close its mist dampened the air he breathed.

The dead boy had just come to the ravine to have fun, Vinny thought. Just a regular kid like him, come to swim and be with his friends, then go home and eat macaroni and cheese and watch TV, maybe play with his dog or wander around after dark.

But he'd done none of that.

Where was he?

Inch by inch Vinny made it to the ledge. He stood, swaying slightly, the tip of his toes one small movement from the precipice.

Far below, Joe-Boy waved his arm back and forth. It was dreamy to see—back and forth, back and forth. He looked so small down there.

For a moment Vinny's mind went blank, as if he were in some trance, some dream where he could so easily lean out and fall and think or feel nothing.

A breeze picked up and moved the trees on the ridgeline, but not a breath of it reached the fifty-foot ledge.

Vinny thought he heard a voice, small and distant. Yes. Something inside him, a tiny voice pleading *Don't do it. Walk away. Just turn and go and walk back down.*

"I can't," Vinny whispered.

You can, you can, you can. Walk back down.

Vinny waited.

And waited.

Joe-Boy yelled, then Starlene, both of them waving.

Then something very strange happened.

Vinny felt at peace. Completely and totally calm and at peace. He had not made up his mind about jumping. But something else inside him had.

Thoughts and feelings swarmed, stinging him: *Jump! Jump! Jump! Jump!*

But deep inside where the peace was, where his mind wasn't, he would not jump. He would walk back down.

No! No, no, no!

Vinny eased down and fingered up some mud and made a cross on his chest, big and bold. He grabbed a leaf, stuck it in his mouth. Be calm, be calm. Don't look down.

After a long pause, he spat the leaf out and rubbed the cross to a blur.

They walked out of the ravine in silence, Starlene, Joe-Boy, and Mo far ahead of him. They hadn't said a word since he'd come down off the trail. He knew what they were thinking. He knew, he knew, he knew.

At the same time the peace was still there. He had no idea what it was. But he prayed it wouldn't leave him now, prayed it wouldn't go away, would never go away, because in there, in that place where the peace was, it didn't matter what they thought.

Vinny emerged from the ravine into a brilliance that surprised him. Joe-Boy, Starlene, and Mo were now almost down to the road.

Vinny breathed deeply and looked up and out over the island. He saw from there a land that rolled away like honey, easing down a descent of rich kikuyu-grass pastureland, flowing from there over vast highlands of brown and green, then, finally, falling massively to the coast and flat blue sea.

He'd never seen anything like it.

Had it always been here? This view of the island?

He stared and stared, then sat, taking it in.

He'd never seen anything so beautiful in all his life.

Mrs. Noonan

He'd seen Mrs. Noonan before, of course.

She was his chemistry teacher's wife. He'd seen her coming and going from their small faculty house. Sometimes he would see her working in her garden or carrying something in from her car or maybe just out walking with Mr. Noonan.

But this time it was different.

Billy Keiffer was in tenth grade—a freaky year, maybe even the freakiest year of his entire life so far.

At his all-boy boarding school up in the island high-country, the air on a clear night was often cool and crisp.

On this particular night Keiffer was out in the cow pasture hiding from Nitt and Johnson. He'd found a place just outside the fence that separated the school from the ranch that edged it. He'd flattened a square of tall grass and was lying on his back with his hands behind his head, thinking of ways he could get Nitt, and Johnson too, for that matter—make their lives as miserable as they'd been making his.

Within ten minutes he figured he'd spent about enough brain cells on those two idiots. Forget them, he thought. My time will come, and when it does I'll know what to do. Sooner or later Nitt will pay. Oh yeah, he's going to pay, all right.

Keiffer dozed a moment, then opened his eyes.

Wow, he thought. Look at the stars. Look how incredibly many there are. Billions.

He listened to the night.

Only a few mosquitoes.

Nothing moved, nothing at all; there wasn't even a breath of breeze.

He bolted up.

What if someone came looking for him? They might. If Mr. Bentley went to his room for some reason. And he wasn't there.

Keiffer peeked over the tall grass.

That's when he saw . . .

Oh.

He hadn't realized he was that close to the faculty bungalows. He stopped breathing.

She was so . . .

Close.

Keiffer gulped in air. He felt his heart leaping up into his throat. His body trembled like a wet dog.

Oh, oh, oh.

The grassy spot was at the top of a small rise that sloped down toward the house. Not forty yards away, framed within the warm yellow square of a window, was Mrs. Noonan. And Keiffer could see perfectly.

She must have turned the light on while he'd been thinking about Nitt, or maybe while he'd dozed off.

She was reading.

Keiffer sank down to where he could just see up over the grass.

She was sitting at one end of a navy blue couch with her legs tucked up under her. A floor lamp illuminated her golden hair. Keiffer already knew her name was Julie. Mr. Noonan had told them that in class. Keiffer guessed she was about twenty-six, since Mr. Noonan was twenty-six. He'd told them that too.

She smiled as she read, one hand holding the book, the other tucked into the fold of her evening kimono, just above her breast.

Keiffer's hands were more than trembling now. Shaking.

It was an accident.

Really. Being there looking into Mr. Noonan's window at his wife was not something he'd come out here to do. He'd only wanted to get away from Nitt and Johnson.

He had to leave.

Now.

But he couldn't move. He couldn't turn away.

Mrs. Noonan took her hand from her kimono to swipe the corner of her eye with a finger. Whatever she was reading was making her smile and cry at the same time. She put her hand back where it had been, inside her kimono.

The vision burned itself into Keiffer's brain.

The window.

The blue sofa.

Her glowing hair.

Her hand.

Mr. Noonan suddenly came into the room.

Keiffer fell back into the grass. He got back up. He'd never seen Mr. Noonan in his pajamas before. Not really pajamas, but a T-shirt and boxer shorts. Mr. Noonan stood behind the sofa with his hand on Mrs. Noonan's shoulder. He leaned down and kissed the top of her head.

Keiffer knew he should get out of there. What he was doing wasn't right. But he couldn't turn away from it, not in a million years.

Mrs. Noonan looked up, smiling. She touched Mr. Noonan's hand, took it and kissed it.

Kissed it and pulled it down.

Keiffer stumbled back. He scrambled to his feet and ran, his heartbeat slamming up in his throat.

Three nights later in the dorm, Nitt and Johnson put centipedes in Keiffer's bed, and in his roommate, Casey's. Casey got stung and screamed like a girl. Keiffer ran out the door, thinking the place was infested.

Nitt and Johnson were in the hall, laughing their heads off, rolling on the floor holding their stomachs.

"You're sick, you stupid freaks!" Keiffer shouted.

Inside the room Casey screamed again.

Johnson was rolling with laughter.

Nitt, trying to stand, pointed at Keiffer. He was practically crying, he was laughing so hard. "You're the freak, Keiffer. You're such a fairy," he said.

Keiffer charged and slammed into him with his shoulder, knocking Nitt to the floor. Nitt landed flat on his back.

"*Ooof!*"

For a moment Nitt couldn't breathe, the air knocked out of him. He sat and stared up in wide-eyed panic. His face started turning red.

Johnson grabbed Keiffer by the neck and threw him out of the way. Keiffer hated Nitt, but he was terrified of Johnson. Keiffer once saw Johnson put a safety pin through the skin on his own arm, grinning at the guys who were watching him. He clipped the pin shut and wore it on his arm until it got infected.

Johnson knelt and thumped Nitt's back. A few long seconds later Nitt caught his breath and gasped.

"You better start running, Keiffer," Johnson said.

Nitt struggled to his knees, his eyes cold. He staggered up, fat fists balled. He stood nearly a foot taller than Keiffer.

"Stay away from me!" Keiffer shouted. They could kill him if they wanted, he didn't care, just get it over with.

Nitt grinned. "You're gonna pay for that, homo."

Every door in the hall was open now, heads peeking out.

Nitt struck so quickly that Keiffer didn't even see it coming. The blow caught him on the side of his head. He stumbled back and fell. White stars speckled his vision and his ears rang.

Nitt kicked him in the stomach and stood over him, a bomb ready to go off if Keiffer said one more word.

Keiffer sat balled up, his hand covering his ear.

Someone yanked Nitt away. All Keiffer saw was a hand grabbing Nitt's shoulder and spinning him around.

"That's enough," Casey said. "I'm getting Mr. Bentley."

Nitt shoved Casey away. "Don't touch me, you faggot!"

Casey backed away and ran down the hall.

"Yeah, go get Mommy," Johnson called after him.

Nitt kicked Keiffer again. "You haven't seen anything yet, Keiffie-babes."

Nitt and Johnson walked away as Casey banged on the dorm master's door. Mr. Bentley wasn't in.

Keiffer waited three nights before sneaking out again. He waited until Casey was asleep. Casey always dozed off before lights-out, which was ten o'clock. He was one of those guys who could get straight As without opening a book almost.

Keiffer crept through the bushes, staying in the shadows out behind the mess hall. His hands started to tremble with anticipation of what he might see. Mrs. Noonan lived with him now, in his mind. He could hardly think of anything else.

He made his way around in back of the faculty bungalows. He found the grassy spot, still mashed down.

But the light in the Noonans' house was off.

His hands stopped trembling. The fantasies began to fade. But he kept hoping.

He waited fifteen minutes and was just about to leave when the light flicked on. And there, in the window, there, there . . .

Julie.

This time her kimono was loosely hung about her. Keiffer was stunned. What is this? What is this *feeling,* this monster feeling?

He nearly had a heart attack when she came to the window, bent down, and looked directly at him.

He froze, stupefied.

But she was only unlatching the window so she could raise it an inch or two.

She sat again on the couch with her book. She opened it and with her free hand gathered up the looseness in the kimono.

Mr. Noonan didn't appear this time. Keiffer stayed until she turned the light off, an hour or thereabouts.

Nothing stirred in the dorm when he returned. Casey still lay as he'd been, facing the wall, dead to the world.

Keiffer fell asleep at about two in the morning, after reliving every memory he could drag up about Mrs. Noonan.

Julie Noonan.

Beautiful Julie Noonan.

A night later he went again. She was lying on the couch talking on the phone.

When he went again two nights after that, the house was dark. He waited nearly an hour, but nothing happened. He knew he shouldn't go there every night, but he couldn't help it. The next night she was there, alone, reading.

His favorite dream was that he was lying on the couch with his head in her lap, and as she read, she stroked his hair and his cheek, leaning down every so often to kiss him. He dreamed about her when he was outside her window. He dreamed about her before falling asleep, and sometimes even had real dreams that were wilder and better than his day-dreams. He dreamed of her in the mess hall when he was at lunch or dinner, looking across the tables to where she sat next to Mr. Noonan.

He went out again that Sunday night.

He could have avoided trouble if he'd been even half alert, but everything around him was consumed in a blur of anticipation.

He was passing behind the mess hall.

"Fairy," someone whispered from the darkness.

He immediately dropped to a squat.

"Yeah, you, Keiffie-babes. What you doing out here?"

Keiffer saw an orange-red glow of light.

A cigarette.

No, two cigarettes.

"Come here," Nitt whispered.

Keiffer stood and walked toward the back of the mess hall. He saw two shadows with red glows leaning against the side of the building.

Johnson and Nitt.

Keiffer squinted. It looked like Johnson was scanning the stars with a pair of binoculars.

"Come on," Nitt said. "We don't bite."

If he ran, he might make it back to the dorm before they caught him. But maybe not too, and if he did run, and they did catch him, it would be worse than just doing what they said.

Panic flared up and inhabited Keiffer's entire body. What if they'd seen him sneaking around before and had been waiting for him? He didn't think they had, but it was possible. Or were they just out stealing a smoke? He'd have to be way more careful in the future.

Nitt and Johnson got up and stood sucking their cigarettes, the embers glowing, then dimming. Nitt flicked his away. It twirled into the darkness and vanished.

"Come closer," he said, softly.

Keiffer took a step.

"Two bits says you were on your way to the pasture, huh? Going out to run naked in the night." He chuckled. "That right?"

"No."

"No?"

He turned to Johnson. "You hear that? The fairy just came out here to go nowhere."

Johnson said nothing, still studying the stars with the binoculars. He sucked his cigarette. "Look at that," he said.

Nitt glanced up. "Satellite."

"Closest thing to a UFO we've seen yet."

Keiffer saw the white pinprick moving across the sky in a pure, clean arc.

Johnson put the binoculars down. "I heard they do that, you know, run naked . . . the fairy guys."

Nitt snickered. "That's really it, isn't it, Keiffie-babes?"

Keiffer said nothing. He should have run when he had the chance.

He bolted.

But they were just as fast.

Nitt grabbed his T-shirt. Keiffer tried to squirm away but Johnson was all over him. They threw him to the ground, facedown, and sat on him.

Nitt whispered in his ear. "Where you going, homo? The party's just warming up."

They turned him over. Nitt unbuttoned Keiffer's jeans and yanked them off. Johnson pulled his T-shirt up over his head and threw it into the weeds.

Nitt, sitting on Keiffer's knees, said to Johnson, "You pull off his underpants. I ain't touching it."

Johnson grinned. "Stand up, faggot."

Keiffer sat, then got to his feet.

"Take 'em off," Johnson said.

Keiffer stared at Johnson. I won't cry, he willed, won't, won't. He bent over and removed his underwear. The burn in his throat swelled. Cry, cry. He crammed it back down inside him.

"Throw them on the roof," Johnson said.

Keiffer tossed his underpants up on top of the mess hall.

"Cute," Nitt said to Johnson.

"Thanks."

It was dark. So what if he was naked? He could make it back to the dorm without being seen. Just wait, and run when the chance came.

"Hold this little pecker's arms up over his head," Nitt said, whispering, trying to keep his voice down.

Johnson grabbed Keiffer's wrists and pulled his arms up.

"Ow!" Keiffer said, trying to wiggle free.

Johnson kneed Keiffer in the butt, and Keiffer stopped.

"I need your weed," Nitt said, taking the cigarette from Johnson's lips. He took a deep drag on it, the tip red-hot. Then he pointed the small fire at Keiffer's face. He grinned, then moved the burning tip down to Keiffer's armpit. He held it so close Keiffer could feel the heat.

"You tell anyone we did this to you and we'll make this part real. Can you imagine it? The stink of burning flesh? The pain in your foul armpit?"

Keiffer said nothing.

"You understand, Keiffie-babes?"

"Yes," Keiffer squeaked.

"Let him go," Nitt said.

Keiffer rubbed his wrists. He felt like a ghost in his nakedness. He bent over, crossed his hands over his crotch.

"What you got to hide, sweetheart? Fairies don't have dongs."

Johnson stifled a laugh.

"What'd you do with my binoculars?" Nitt asked.

Johnson picked them up, brushed the dirt off, and handed them to Nitt.

Nitt packed them into a case and threw the strap over his shoulder. "Let's go," he said.

They took Keiffer out into the pasture. He could see Mr. Noonan's house. The light was on, but no one was in sight. Keiffer turned away quickly, not wanting Nitt or Johnson to even have a clue about the window. Oh God, what they would do if they knew about Mrs. Noonan.

Nitt stopped out in the middle of the pasture. "This should do, huh, Keiffie?"

Keiffer glanced around to see if there were any cows, or worse, bulls. But he could see only dark shadows of trees and bushes and the few lights on campus.

"We're going to be watching," Nitt said. "And we're going to be real disappointed if you don't have a good time out here, you know? So just go on and play with yourself, fairybabes, flit around like Tarzan or Peter Pan or whoever it is you want to be."

He tapped Keiffer's shoulder as if they were good old buds from way back.

They left, their laughter slicing the stillness.

Keiffer noticed for the first time that he was cold. He crossed his arms. What do I do? What?

He looked back toward the school, the faculty bungalows.

Oh, no, now she was there.

In the window.

Keiffer felt a crybaby-burn rise in his throat again. Tears spilled from his eyes. He wiped them away quickly.

Crouching low, he made his way back, slipping around the mess hall the opposite way. It meant he would have to sprint across the quad to get to the dorm, out in the open. But he'd have to take that chance. Nitt might be waiting if he went back the way he'd come.

Keiffer stood at the edge of the building, half in the bushes. No one was in sight. He stepped out, started creeping into the quad.

"What the hell are you doing out here, Mr. Keiffer?"

Keiffer's heart nearly flew out of his throat. He staggered back. Mr. Bentley was sitting on the mess hall steps.

"I . . . I . . ."

Mr. Bentley stood. "Jesus, you're stark naked."

"But—"

At that moment Nitt and Johnson came out of the shadows behind Mr. Bentley. They stopped short and ditched their cigarettes the second they saw him.

Mr. Bentley turned.

Nitt shot Keiffer a glare that said, If you breathe one word about anything, you'll be dead in an hour.

"What the hell is going on here?" Mr. Bentley said. "Have you all gone mad? No one's supposed to be out of the dorm after ten. You know that."

Nitt, in his most agreeable voice, said, "We've just got senioritis, Mr. Bentley. You know how that is, don't you?"

Mr. Bentley shook his head.

Keiffer wondered if Nitt thought Mr. Bentley might have seen the cigarettes. Nitt said, "We were just playing a joke on Keiffer, sir."

Mr. Bentley looked at Keiffer. "Taking him outside buck naked, you mean?"

"Yeah, just a little joke."

Mr. Bentley eyed Nitt. "Mr. Nitt, you're so full of it you're actually funny. Get back to the dorm, all of you. Jesus."

Keiffer ran ahead. If stupid Nitt thought his butt was saved, he could think again. All Keiffer needed was time and a killer idea. Oh yeah. Time and a killer idea.

The following Saturday night everyone was in the common room watching some old movie. Keiffer, Nitt, and Johnson sat in the library with their books spread out around them. Mr. Bentley had written them up for two hours of study hall as punishment. Thankfully, Mr. Bentley had kept the nakedness part to himself.

Keiffer sat alone at one of the computer tables, the lit screen blank in front of him. He had to write a report on Pearl Harbor for history. Nitt and Johnson were studying at tables of their own, farther away. But Keiffer could see them from where he sat. Two seventh graders were at another table. Mr. Paine, this week's study hall monitor, was at a desk up toward the door, keeping an eye on things.

Keiffer typed: *On December 7, 1941, the Japanese attacked Pearl Harbor.*

He stopped and thought.

And thought.

Of Mrs. Noonan.

It was hopeless. *He* was hopeless.

He peeked up at Mr. Paine, then over at Nitt, whose head was resting on his arms, folded over the top of the desk. Johnson was slouched down reading some book.

Keiffer opened a new page on the screen.

Dear Julie,

He peeked up again. He could feel a tingling inside him just at the thought of writing her a letter. He'd never *give* it to her, of course. But just to write it . . .

I know you don't know me, but you've probably seen me around. Who I am doesn't matter. What does matter is that I think you are the most beautiful woman I have ever seen in my life. I think about you every night and every day. I can't STOP. It's like I'm in a dream and you and I are the only people in the world. Sometimes I think about kissing you. I've never kissed anyone in my life. But if I could kiss you, I would never want to kiss anyone else ever again. I love you more than anyone ever could. I don't know how to say it any stronger than that. I love you, I love you, I love you.

From your secret admirer

Keiffer read it and smiled. He read it again and again.

He looked up. Nitt was still dozing and Johnson still reading. He hit the print command and held his breath as the printer hummed it out.

He snatched it up and read it one more time, then folded it and hid it in the pages of his math book for later.

The next night in the dorm after dinner, when everyone else was in their rooms doing homework, Keiffer leaned back in his chair and stretched.

Casey was reading a novel in Spanish, lying on his bed with headphones on. Probably listening to jazz, Keiffer thought. Casey was a little weird, but a nice guy. He kept to himself. Avoided all trouble. All he wanted in the world was to get into MIT with a perfect record.

Keiffer stood and Casey looked up.

"Just going out for a walk," Keiffer said. "I'm falling asleep."

Casey nodded and turned back to his book.

Keiffer went a different way this time, skirting the back of the mess hall. It was full dark out, no moon. The air was cool and it smelled like ginger.

And she was there, alone in the room.

Keiffer figured Mr. Noonan must have a different place in the house where he worked, or read, or graded papers.

Mrs. Noonan was talking on the phone again. She wore a T-shirt this time, and Keiffer wondered if she had anything on under it. In his mind she didn't. He remembered the letter he'd written and thought of how he'd felt as he'd written it and how it was true to the last drop. He should give it to her. Secretly.

A mosquito hummed near his ear and he slapped it. *Whack!*

Mrs. Noonan looked up.

She reached toward the lamp and shut it off.

Keiffer froze and stared at the darkened house.

A light appeared, a flashlight shining through the screen. Mumbling voices.

Keiffer staggered back and stumbled away. He fell and got up and raced through the weeds and grass and trees, sprinting back to the dorm and his room, where he slammed the door and leaned back against it, then fell on his bed, gasping.

Casey, still reading, looked up.

"Just . . . just ran a bit," Keiffer said. "To wake up."

Casey shook his head.

A moment later he said, "Your friend Nitt was here looking for you."

Keiffer didn't answer. Immediately he got up and checked his stash to see if Nitt had taken his cookies that his mom had sent. There had been fourteen left. Now there were only five.

"He also messed around over at your desk," Casey added.

Keiffer checked there too. Everything was out of place, but nothing seemed to be missing. "What did he want?" he asked.

"What does he ever want? Food."

Keiffer scowled and straightened his desk. His

hands still shook from the shock of almost getting caught. He had no idea, just no idea, that sound could carry so far in the night outside Mrs. Noonan's window.

It took him hours to fall asleep.

Moments after he finally did, he bolted awake.

He turned on his desk lamp and grabbed his math book.

The letter was gone.

On Tuesday Keiffer took the biggest chance he'd ever taken in his life. It was so big he wondered what was happening to him. He'd never acted this way before. He'd *thought* about doing things like this, many times, but he'd never actually followed up on anything.

This time he did.

Because the killer thought had arrived.

He pretended to be sick and spent the day in bed. But while everyone was at class, he crept over to the senior dorm and went into Nitt and Johnson's room. Nothing was ever locked. Which in this case was great. He had to find that letter and tear it up.

The room stank. It was like Nitt and Johnson had a stash of really gross laundry somewhere.

Keiffer couldn't find the letter.

In fact, Nitt had nothing at all of interest on or in his desk or clothes drawers or closet. He didn't

even have one picture of anyone on his cork-
board. He didn't have a stereo, a clock, or even a
pencil sharpener. Keiffer frowned.

But there was the one other thing he'd come to
get. And that was way more than enough.

Nitt's binoculars.

They were high up on the top shelf of Nitt's
closet in their frayed black case. Someone had
scribbled *Nitt, U.S. Army Infantry* on the strap.

Keiffer grabbed the case and left.

That night, after he heard Casey breathing
deeply, Keiffer threw the binocular case over his
shoulder and peeked out into the quiet hall.

One light was on down near Mr. Bentley's
apartment.

He hurried to the door and went out into the
night, feeling an electric thing inside him even
stronger and more driving than before. It raced
through him. Charged every nerve in his body so
that the trembling in his hands took hold again,
and even before he'd gotten halfway to the grassy
hiding place outside Mrs. Noonan's window, he
had to stop and breathe.

Breathe and think.

All right, settle down.

He gripped the binoculars.

She was reading.

She was wearing the kimono.

Keiffer couldn't keep the eyepiece still.

Wow.

Wow, wow, wow.

She was even more beautiful up close—so close that he kissed her, tasted her lips, felt them so soft and damp and smooth, her hands now caressing his face and hair.

Keiffer watched her read for fifteen minutes, exploring every inch of her—her eyes, her smile, her hair, her body, everything—until she put her hand inside her kimono above her breast, as was her habit.

When she did that, put her hand there, in that spot, Keiffer lowered the binoculars. His ears quivered with the pain of it all. He could never have her to himself. Never. She loved Mr. Noonan. Not him. She would hate him if she knew he was out there spying. She would think he was nothing but some sick, dorky tenth grader.

"But it's not like that," he whispered.

He looked one more time, then lowered the binoculars and put them down in the grass, near the case.

Do it now, he thought.

He coughed, very lightly, as if trying to stifle it.

The light in the house went out.

Keiffer flattened down into the grass.

In seconds Mr. Noonan burst out the back door with the flashlight, combing the trees and pasture, the beam passing just over Keiffer's head.

"Who's out there?" Mr. Noonan shouted.

When the beam moved off into the pasture, Keiffer got up and ran for his life.

The next morning Nitt got called into the headmaster's office. At noon in the mess hall word spread like floodwater. Nitt had been peeping into Noonan's house at night. More than once, everyone whispered. Mrs. Noonan had heard him out there. Mr. Noonan had found his binoculars.

That afternoon Keiffer was trying to concentrate in English class when a seventh grader came in with a note. Mr. Ellis read it, then strolled down the aisle to the back of the room and gave it to Keiffer.

Keiffer opened it.

He looked at it and sat for a moment without moving, then stood and gathered his books. All eyes watched him leave.

He stepped out under gray and white clouds. Rain fell like mist as he headed across the green grass toward the headmaster's office.

Mr. Noonan was there. And Mr. Bentley. And Mr. Toms, the headmaster, a burly, red-haired man who rarely smiled.

Mr. Toms pointed to a chair and Keiffer sat. His hands started to tremble. He sat on them.

He'd been caught. It was over.

He waited for someone to say something.

To call his parents.

To tell him to go back to his room and start packing.

It was so quiet that he could hear Mr. Toms breathing.

Mr. Bentley leaned forward, his elbows on his knees. In one hand he held a folded piece of paper.

"Mr. Keiffer," he said, then paused.

Keiffer stared at the floor.

"I assume you've heard what happened with Mr. Nitt."

"Yes sir."

Mr. Bentley nodded. "When we went through his belongings, we found something that he swore was yours. He said he took it from your room."

Mr. Bentley handed Keiffer the folded paper. "Did you write this?"

Keiffer took the letter. He unfolded it and pretended to read it. He willed his hand to stop trembling.

The letter shook.

"Mr. Keiffer?"

"No sir, this isn't mine. I don't know anyone named Julie."

Keiffer kept his eyes on the letter, afraid to look up. He felt sick.

Mr. Bentley went on. "Remember the night I caught you out buck naked?"

Keiffer winced. He wanted to crawl out of the room. He could feel the blood rush to his face.

"Yes sir," he whispered.

"I've got to say, I was rather stunned to see you like that. But then Mr. Nitt and Mr. Johnson showed up and said they'd just played a practical joke on you. Was that true, what they said? Did they strip you and take you outside?"

"Yes sir, they did. They took me out into the cow pasture."

"And . . ."

Keiffer looked up. He shrugged. "Nothing. I just walked back. That's when . . . when I saw you."

"Those two boys do that kind of thing to you a lot?"

"No sir. I mean they never did that before. They do plenty of . . . of other stuff, but not that."

"What other stuff?"

"Beat me up. Steal food. Put centipedes in my bed."

Mr. Bentley paused, thinking.

Keiffer glanced up.

Mr. Bentley straightened and turned to Mr. Toms and Mr. Noonan. "Well, you know how the boys are. It's not the first time something like that has happened."

Keiffer glanced at Mr. Toms, who sat with his arms crossed, scowling, tapping a finger on his arm. "What's your point, Mr. Bentley?" Mr. Toms said.

"My point is that Mr. Nitt has had it in for Mr. Keiffer for some time. Mr. Keiffer's roommate told me about the centipedes. I've no reason to believe that trying to pin the letter on Mr. Keiffer was any different. Besides, I just can't see Mr. Keiffer writing something like that. And we did find it in Mr. Nitt's room."

Mr. Toms, his arms still crossed, looked directly into Keiffer's eyes. He was mulling something over.

Finally he said, "Did you write that letter, son?"

Keiffer felt as if his mind were a total blank. The thoughts and words he needed to tell the truth were just not there. Part of him wanted to get it out, get the whole thing over. But a stronger part of him was terrified.

"I don't know anyone named Julie," he mumbled.

Mr. Bentley sat back in his chair.

Mr. Noonan's silence was almost too much for Keiffer to bear.

"I'm going to ask you one more time, son," Mr. Toms said. "Is that letter yours? This is very important. Expelling a boy from this school is no small thing. Now I want you to tell me—did Mr. Nitt take that letter from your room like he said he did?"

Keiffer's thoughts raced.

He saw, in his mind, the hot cigarette nearly burning his armpit, and he saw himself stripped naked in the pasture. He saw Nitt kicking him in the hallway, and the hate and rage in his eyes. He saw him shoving Casey and calling him a homo. And the cookie box with the missing cookies, and the centipedes in his bed, and the stolen letter, his letter, his, the private one he wrote that was meant for no one else to see but himself, no one, ever.

"Son?"

Keiffer could not speak. He was gone. He knew it. Gone, gone, gone. He'd pack tonight probably. Call his mom.

There was a long silence.

He'd tell them the truth.

Keiffer felt himself swaying, just slightly. He could hardly keep from passing out.

Tell them.

Keiffer shook his head. "No sir. I did not write that letter."

Mr. Toms studied him. A long, thoughtful look.

Finally he said, "I'm inclined to believe you."

Keiffer looked up, then down. Then up.

Mr. Toms breathed deeply, thinking. He rubbed a hand over his face. A truck shifted gears out on the road, the sound of the engine falling, then rising again.

Mr. Toms stood. "You can go, Mr. Keiffer."

Keiffer stayed where he was.

Tell him, he thought. Tell him now.

Keiffer stood and left the room.

In less than twenty-four hours Nitt was history.

Put on a plane to Honolulu.

Expelled.

For days Keiffer felt awful. He didn't know what he'd meant to do, but getting Nitt kicked out of school wasn't part of it. He'd just wanted to . . . to get him. That's all. Just get him.

And he did, better than he'd ever even imagined, and that felt good.

Yes.

No, it didn't.

He would tell. To lie was wrong.

But what did it matter anymore? He was going crazy anyway. He was already a whack. Mrs. Noonan had made him that way.

All right, he decided. I'll do it. I'll tell. Just not right now. But soon.

Keiffer kept more to himself than ever after that, going a little crazier every day, he thought. His life was one big mess. He waffled back and forth many times a day: Tell, now. No, it's done, let it be.

But above all else he had to get Mrs. Noonan out of his mind. If it hadn't been for her, none of this would have happened.

He stopped eating for a while. Then started again, nibbling. Never laughed or smiled. Never tried to talk to anyone. Just sank down into himself.

And, eventually, he even began to stop dreaming about Mrs. Noonan.

But then . . .

He was outside in the quad one sunny afternoon when he saw Mr. and Mrs. Noonan walking toward him. They were holding hands.

Maybe his mind was playing tricks on him, but Keiffer thought Mr. Noonan seemed to have taken on a new way of looking at him since that meeting in Mr. Toms's office. It was really weird, because Keiffer thought it was a look of admiration, almost as if Mr. Noonan respected him for having had the guts to talk with Mr. Toms the way he had. Stand up to Nitt's lie like he did.

Even so, Keiffer found it almost impossible to look Mr. Noonan in the eye. He'd glance at him and turn away quickly. That's how it usually went.

Mr. Noonan smiled as he and Mrs. Noonan approached.

They stopped.

"How's it going, Keiffer?" Mr. Noonan said.

"All right."

"Staying out of trouble?"

"Yes sir."

Mr. Noonan grinned and tapped Keiffer's shoulder. "Good man. Say, have you ever met my wife? I know you've seen her around, but I don't think you've actually met, have you?"

Keiffer shook his head. "No sir."

He couldn't look at Mrs. Noonan either.

Just seeing her reminded him of Nitt, and his own private letter, the one Mr. Toms had in his desk drawer. Just thinking that made him cringe. No, he couldn't look at her. Mrs. Noonan was a bad dream for him now.

"Well, then," Mr. Noonan said. "Julie, meet Billy

Keiffer. He's a fine young man and not a bad chemist."

"Hi, Billy," she said.

Her voice so soothing.

Saying his name.

So soft and light.

He forced himself to look up.

She was smiling, her head tilted slightly. She reached out to shake hands.

Keiffer hesitated, then took her hand.

Took Mrs. Noonan's hand.

The hand.

There was nothing else in the world now.

Nothing.

Forty Bucks

Shane, a tenth grader at Farrington, and Jimmy, a seventeen-year-old Kaimuki High School dropout, were just about to lock up the Taco Bell on Kalanimoku Street when the old man came in.

This old guy wasn't old like a one-soft-taco-and-low-fat-milk kind of old, but more like a two-bean-burritos-with-no-onions-and-ice-tea old guy. Tired, puffy bulges like tiny hammocks hung under his eyes, and above, at a slight angle, he wore a brand-new black felt cowboy hat with a gray feather hatband.

"Mister, we wen' close, already," Shane called from behind the counter. Jimmy was in the back mopping the floor.

The old man smiled and nodded and went on over to sit at a table as if Shane had said, "Come on in and have a seat."

"Hey, mister, I said . . . tst."

Shane frowned and shook his head and walked out around the counter to look into the night to see if anyone else was hanging around out there. When he saw no one—no cars, no nothing—he started to go over and lock the door but decided not to because he still had to get the old man out of there.

Shane went to where the man had set himself down and, resting his hands on the table, leaned forward and gently said, "Mister . . . we wen' shut down, already. You gotta go. We closed."

The old man scratched his slightly whiskery chin and thought a moment. *"Una cerveza fría, gracias. Solo una cerveza fría."*

Shane looked dumbly at the man, then straightened up. "Hey, Jimmy," he called. "Try come."

Jimmy came out carrying the mop. "What? Who's that? We stay close."

"I know that, but he don't. You tell him."

Jimmy leaned on his mop and said, "We stay close, old man. No food."

The old man yawned, rubbed the back of his neck, and said, *"¿Qué cerveza tiene? No, olvídelo. No importa. Deme lo que tenga frío."*

"What he said?" Jimmy asked.

Shane shrugged. Wasn't Japanese. Wasn't Chinese or Filipino. But it did sort of sound like Mrs. Medeiros when she got mad. "Maybe it's Portuguese," Shane said.

"Portuguese? You know Portuguese?"

"No."

Jimmy frowned. "How about sign language? You know that?"

"Only the sign on the door that says Closed at 11 P.M."

"So what we going do?"

Shane and Jimmy stood there a moment studying the man who sat there smiling up at them. *"¿Hay algún problema?"* the man said.

"Maybe he wants a burrito."

"Well, then he going say 'burrito,' ah?"

Jimmy shrugged. "We couldn't make him one anyways. Gotta turn everything back on again. And I ain't doing that."

The old man reached into his shirt pocket and pulled out a wad of crisp, clean twenty-dollar bills. He peeled one off and put it on the table. *"¿Es suficiente?"* he said.

"Put that away," Shane said. "We ain't selling anything. We closed."

When the old man looked blank-eyed at him, Shane added, "No likey talk, no likey money. Closed, I said. *Pau.* Time for go home, already."

The man frowned and peeled off another twenty-dollar bill and put it on top of the one already on the table. *"¿Basta con esto? ¿Cuánto cuesta una cerveza?"*

"Hoo, the guy rich," Jimmy said. "For forty bucks I make him one burrito triple supreme."

Shane scowled at Jimmy.

"Kay-okay," Jimmy said. "Just joking."

Headlights from a pickup truck pulling into the parking lot glared in the window. The driver gunned the engine, then shut it down. The lights went off.

"Aw, man," Jimmy said. "Now we got more people coming in. Did you lock the door?"

"No. I was waiting to get this old guy out."

Two boys about eighteen years old got out of the truck and slammed their way through the door into Taco Bell. One was kind of fat and the other tall and lanky, with a tattoo of a knife with dripping blood just above his elbow. The two boys glared at Shane and Jimmy. The bloody-knife one noticed the forty bucks on the table and said, "You buying, old man?"

The old man smiled up at him. *"Ellos no me entienden. ¿Hablan español? ¿Les puede decir que solo quiero una cerveza?"* Then he made drinking motions with his hand.

When the old man said "español," Shane knew he was speaking Spanish because he'd heard his older brother say that over and over last year when his brother was taking Spanish in the eleventh grade. *"Hablo español, amigo,"* he'd said about fifty thousand times. No, *"Yo hablo español, amigo."*

"¿Cerveza?" the old man said again.

The tattoo boy looked at his friend, then at Shane and Jimmy. "What he said?"

Jimmy said quickly, "Nothing. Who can understand him? Anyways, we're closed."

The tall boy said, "Door's open, so you open, and we hungry."

"If you don't believe me, look at the sign on the door," Shane said. "We closed fifteen minutes, already."

The old man, looking as if he'd decided that he wasn't going to be understood and was wasting his time by hanging around, shook his head and got up to leave.

The fat boy glanced at him when he stood up, then turned back and got in Shane's face, so close Shane could smell his stink breath.

Shane took a step back.

The fat boy pulled out a long switchblade and flicked it open and grinned when Shane turned white as a boiled octopus.

When the old man saw the knife his eyes squinted down so slightly you almost didn't notice any movement in them at all. Slowly he sat back down, his eyes pinned on the knife. He put the two twenty-dollar bills back on the table as if he'd changed his mind about leaving.

The fat boy poked Shane's chest with his finger. "My fren said Taco Bell is open, know what I'm saying?"

Shane nodded. "Yeah, but—"

"You like me stick you wit' this, or wot?"

Shane clammed up.

"Eh, eh, eh," the old man said to the fat boy. *"No se ponga así. Tranquilícese. Les invito a una cerveza."*

"Whatchoo talking? German, or wot?" the fat boy said, folding the blade back into the handle and putting the knife into his pocket. "Hey, Jojo, this guy talking German."

"Not German, you stupit. That's Russian," Jojo the tattoo boy said.

"Russian? No kidding? How come got one Russian fut in Taco Bell?"

"Shuddup, who cares. Hey, you two. Make us some food."

Jimmy hurried back over to the counter and started to turn everything back on.

The fat boy swept his hand over the table, grabbing up the old man's forty dollars. "I could use this," he said, slouching over toward Jojo. The old man followed him with his eyes.

"Whatchoo looking?" Jojo said, glaring at the old man.

The old man kept staring, didn't even blink.

"Futhead," Jojo mumbled after trying to stare the old man down and losing. He and the fat boy went over to a booth near the front window and slumped down into it and started mumbling about something or other.

Shane eased back around the counter to help Jimmy. "Maybe we should call the police," he whispered.

"No, just make some tacos or something. If we call the police, these guys going come back again . . . and then we going had it."

Shane nodded. Maybe Jimmy was right.

Together they brought out some trays of cheese
and refried beans and sliced lettuce and tomatoes
and hamburger meat.

"Whatchoo like eat?" Jimmy called out to the
two boys.

"Six tacos and six burrito supremes," the guy
named Jojo said.

"And two root beers," the fat guy added. "Big
Gulps."

"Big Gulp is 7-Eleven," Jimmy said. "Anyways,
we don't have root beer."

"Hey! I said I like root beer, and no make smart
mout' or you going be sorry, you stupit taco flipper." The fat guy laughed at what he thought was a
pretty clever insult, taco flipper.

Jimmy whispered to Shane, "How we going get
root beer?"

"How should I know? Maybe go across the
street to Foodland. You got any money?"

"Two dollars, about."

"Get some more from the cash register then,"
Shane said.

"What if when I open it that guy comes over
and takes the money like he took that old man's
money?"

Shane thought about that, then searched his
own pockets. "Here, I got another dollar. Just get
three dollars' worth of root beer and get back over
here as fast as you can."

When Jimmy started for the door, Jojo looked
up. "Hey! Where you t'ink you going?"

"Get some root beer."

Jojo laughed. "Hey, Wayne. He going get you some root beer."

The fat guy, Wayne, chuckled and slapped his knee. "You walk out that door, taco flipper, and you going meet Mr. Blade." He laughed some more and patted his pocket where Mr. Blade waited.

Jimmy inched back behind the counter.

Just then the old man got up and walked over to the table where Jojo and Wayne sat. He sat down next to Wayne, the guy who had taken his forty dollars. *"Creo que empiezo a comprender. Sois un par de golfos. Y estáis molestando a estos jóvenes."*

"Get out of here, you stupit Russian fut," Wayne said, scowling at the old man. He slid farther away, closer to the window.

"Devolvedme el dinero y marchaos en paz."

"Where you t'ink you are, ah? Speak English."

Jojo was grinning, as if he was enjoying seeing Wayne squirm. "He's telling you how handsome you are, Wayne. I think he likes you." Jojo whooped, and Wayne gave him a stink scowl.

"What's that old guy telling them?" Jimmy whispered, both of them watching from behind the counter.

"I don't know," Shane said. "But I can tell you this: he's nuts. Those two going cut him up and eat him alive. We gotta call the police."

Jimmy nodded and inched over toward the phone. One step, two.

"What you punks doing back there?" Jojo called. "Where's our food?"

"Coming right up," Jimmy said, leaping away from the phone.

The old man sat staring at Wayne, which made Wayne squirm even more. "Get off this seat, futhead, before I crack and pop you."

The man put his hand out, open, waiting for his forty dollars.

"I think he like that money back," Jojo said.

"Shhh," Wayne spat. "It's mines now."

The old man waited, still staring.

Wayne snapped and whipped the back of his hand at the old man's face.

Quick as a whip, the old man grabbed Wayne's fist and held it in a viselike grip. Wayne grimaced, his eyes wild.

Shane and Jimmy froze, their mouths gaping open.

Jojo laughed, holding his stomach and sliding down in his seat.

"Como dije, lo mejor es que os marcháis," the old man said calmly. *"Pero primero devolvedme mi dinero."*

Wayne struggled, trying to pull his hand away, but the old man held on. Wayne couldn't break loose. His face grew red, his eyes burning with menace. "You had it, old man. I going drag your bones out of here tonight."

"Come on, Wayne," Jojo said. "That's only one old gramps. You no can take 'um, or wot?"

Wayne reached toward the old man with his free hand, but the man twisted the wrist he was gripping and Wayne's head fell to the table. "Ow, ow! Let go! I going kill you! Let go!"

"Call Mrs. Medeiros," Jimmy whispered frantically. "Ask her what we should do. Quick!"

Shane hurried over to the phone, took it off the hook, and hid down behind the counter. He dialed Mrs. Medeiros, who owned the Taco Bell on Kalanimoku Street. The phone rang and rang. Five times, six.

She answered on the seventh ring. "What?" she said, half-awake.

"Mrs. Medeiros, this is Shane. We got a problem."

"What problem? What time is it? Where are you?"

"I'm here. Taco Bell. It's eleven-thirty."

"What's the problem?"

"This old guy came in, but then these other two guys came in, and they're starting to fight. What should we do?"

"Call the police, use your brain. That's why I made you assistant manager. I'll be right down. You call the police." She hung up.

"She said call the police," Shane whispered to Jimmy, who didn't know whether to listen to Shane or watch the fight or make tacos and burritos or run for it.

Wayne yelped in pain and Shane peeked up

over the counter. The old man was still sitting there with Wayne's head mashed down onto the table.

Jojo slid out of the booth and stood up, his bloody-knife tattoo stabbing out like trouble. He didn't seem to know what to do. He glanced over at Shane and Jimmy and saw Shane still holding the phone. "Who you calling? Put that down. Now!"

Shane dropped the receiver. It broke when it hit the tile floor. Part of it bounced around on the end of the cord.

Jojo looked back at Wayne, then scowled when outside he saw a police car's blue lights flashing behind a Corvette stopped in front of the Taco Bell. Two cops were getting out to give some speeder a ticket. "Tst," Jojo spat. "Hurry it up! Gimme the food."

Shane and Jimmy went to work, faster even than they ever did when the place was crushed with customers. In seconds they had the six burrito supremes and six tacos wrapped up in paper and in a sack. They slid the sack out onto the counter, keeping the counter between them and Jojo, who rushed toward them with pinched and angry eyes. "Where's the root beer?" he said.

"We— we—" Jimmy stuttered.

"Shuddup! Gimme some cups."

Shane pointed to the pop dispenser.

Jojo grabbed two large paper cups and filled

them with ice that shot down noisily. "Wayne, let's go!" he said, filling the cups with Coke. He put lids on them and grabbed two straws.

Wayne all this time jerked around, still trying to get free, still with his head mashed down onto the table because the old man was twisting his arm so hard. Outside, the cops were making the Corvette driver spread-eagle against his car.

"Come on!" Jojo shouted to Wayne. "Stop fooling around."

But Wayne couldn't break free.

Jojo looked at the police, then back at Wayne, then hurried out alone. He fired up his truck and drove slowly out of there with the six burrito supremes, six tacos, and two large Cokes.

Shane ran over and locked the door.

The old man smiled when he saw Shane do that and let Wayne the fat boy go.

Wayne sprang up and leaped over the table and jumped out of the booth on the other side. He stood facing the old man, rubbing his wrist. His small mongoose eyes darted around, searching for Jojo, but there was only Shane, Jimmy, and the old man. Slowly he backed away, then turned and ran for the door.

But it was locked now. And you needed a key to get out.

"Unlock this door!" he yelled, banging on it with his fists, then slamming against it with his shoulder.

Shane and Jimmy didn't move. The old man kept smiling.

Wayne whipped out Mr. Blade and flipped him open. "I said open the door, you deaf?"

"Hijo, creo que es mejor que me devolváis el dinero," the old man said.

"Shuddup! I don't speak Russian, you stupit." Wayne started toward the old man with his knife but stopped when another set of headlights flashed into the parking lot.

"Man, where are all these people coming from?" Jimmy mumbled.

"It's Mrs. Medeiros," Shane whispered.

Wayne, seeing the car pull up and, also, for the first time seeing the flashing blue police lights, ran toward Shane and Jimmy, looking for a back door. But the old man stepped in his way and grabbed his shirt as he ran by. *"Dinero,"* he said. *"Dólares."*

Wayne spat in his face.

Boom! Wayne was on the floor, one arm twisted up behind him and the old man's knee jabbing into the small of his back. Wayne winced in pain. "I'm gonna kill . . . *ahhh!"*

Jimmy gaped, not believing the old man could do what he was doing. Shane saw Mrs. Medeiros at the door, fumbling in her purse for her keys. He jumped up and over the counter and hurried to unlock the door.

Wayne thrashed and gasped on the floor.

The old man, tired now of playing around,

twisted the knife out of Wayne's hand and kicked it under the counter. Then he reached into Wayne's pocket and took back his forty dollars and let Wayne go.

Wayne stumbled to his feet and took a swing at the old man but missed by a mile.

Shane had the door open now, and Mrs. Medeiros yelled, "Hold it! Stay where you are!"

But Wayne ran out the back, shoving Jimmy back against the refried-bean tray as he ran by.

"Aw, man," Jimmy said, pulling his hand out of the gooey muck.

"You!" Mrs. Medeiros called to the old man. "Whatchoo in here making trouble for? Shane, how come the police out there an' not inside here? What's going on here?"

"It was those other guys, not this old man," Shane said.

"What other guys? I only saw one."

"There was one more."

The old man pushed up the brim of his hat with his finger. *"Muchachos, ahora sí que necesito esa cerveza,"* he said.

Mrs. Medeiros scowled at him. Then to Shane and Jimmy she said, "You boys get to work and close this place down," and Shane and Jimmy did as she said.

She went over and sat at a table and motioned for the old man to sit down across from her, which he did. *"¿Pero qué quiere?"* she asked him in his language.

The old man smiled, broad and full. He took off his hat and covered his heart with it. *"Señora, yo solo quería una cerveza, eso es todo. Solamente una cerveza."*

Mrs. Medeiros studied him a moment. Then she, too, smiled and the two of them went on in the foreign language that Shane and Jimmy could not understand while they swashed and clanked around behind the counter.

"Shane, Jimmy," Mrs. Medeiros called. "I'll be right back. Let this old man sit here while I'm gone." She got up and headed for the door with her keys jingling.

Outside, the cops were easing the handcuffed Corvette driver into the backseat of the police car. Mrs. Medeiros walked out just as they drove away with him.

"I gotta get a better job," Jimmy mumbled.

"Why?"

"Why? This place is too dangerous, man. Too crazy."

"Dangerous? It's Taco Bell, for crying out loud."

"Yeah, but one of these days some crazy going come in here and freak out and somebody going really get hurt and I don't want it to be me."

"Ain't going be you. Why somebody going hurt you? Us guys, we nothing to anyone who comes in here. We just like the pop machine or the garbage can. They don't see us. We just workers, part of the machinery. Crazy guys want more glory than us."

Jimmy looked at Shane, then shook his head. "You more crazy than the crazies, you know?"

Shane laughed and looked up as Mrs. Medeiros came back in carrying two bottles of beer. She took them over to the table and handed one to the old man, and the two of them talked and laughed and drank beer together like a couple of old friends from way back.

After a while Mrs. Medeiros called to Jimmy, "Try bring me one paper and envelope from the office."

Jimmy got them and brought them out. Mrs. Medeiros pointed to the old man with her chin, and Jimmy put the paper and envelope down in front of him. Mrs. Medeiros dug a pen out of her purse.

While the old man wrote something on the paper, Mrs. Medeiros said to Jimmy, "This man is from Spain. He's staying at the Waikiki Beachcomber. He said he was dragged here by his son and daughter-in-law as a retirement gift, when what he really wanted was just to stay home and work in his garden. But his son always thinks he knows what's best." Mrs. Medeiros chuckled to herself. "Sounds like my husband . . . Anyway, all this man wanted was a beer."

Jimmy said, "But Taco Bell don't sell no beer."

Mrs. Medeiros shook her head. "This is why you should have stayed in school. Your mind needs more exercise."

Jimmy looked down at his hands, and Mrs. Medeiros added, "He thought this place looked like a cantina."

"It looks like the Alamo," Jimmy said.

Mrs. Medeiros studied him a long moment, then with a sigh said, "Why don't you just go finish up so we can all go home to bed."

The old man finished his beer and got up to leave. He whispered something to Mrs. Medeiros and handed her the envelope.

"Buenas noches, muchachos," the old man said, tipping his hat and heading toward the front door with Mrs. Medeiros. *"Que os vaya bien."* He chuckled and vanished into the night.

"Weird," Jimmy said.

Shane agreed, "Weird, but pretty cool, too. The way he shame that punk Wayne."

"Yeah, that was awesome."

Mrs. Medeiros handed Shane the envelope. "This is for you two," she said. "Lock up this time, okay? I'm going home, already. This business going put me in an early grave."

Mrs. Medeiros left, and Shane and Jimmy studied the envelope.

"What it says on the front?" Jimmy asked.

"Para mis valientes amigos," Shane read slowly, stumbling over the strange words.

"What's that mean?"

"I only recognize *amigos,* which means 'friends,' I think."

"In Russian?"

"Not Russian, you idiot. Spanish. All this time you thought it was Russian?"

Jimmy shrugged. "That's what those punks said."

"Jeese."

"Open the envelope," Jimmy said, and Shane tore the end off.

Inside Shane found the two twenty-dollar bills and a note that he read slowly. *El mundo necesita más muchachos trabajadores como vosotros. Os ruego que aceptéis este dinero.* And it was signed *Vuestro amigo, Manuel Rodríguez Martín, comisario de policía (retirado), Valladolid, España.*

"You understand any of it?" Jimmy asked.

"Well, I heard *muchachos* before, that means 'boys,' I think. And there's *amigo* again."

"He gave us this money?" Jimmy asked.

"Looks like it."

"Hoo, maybe I'll keep this job after all."

"See, I told you. We're just part of the machinery. This is like a tip, like oil for the engine that runs the place, know what I mean?"

"No, but what we going do when those two punks Jojo and Wayne come back? We going die then."

"They not going bother us."

"How come you say that?"

"Because number one, Wayne going be mad at Jojo for run out on him, and number two, we never went rat on 'um."

"Whatchoo mean 'rat'?"

"We didn't call the police. We handled it our-self."

"That's because the phone broke."

"So? They don't know that."

Jimmy thought about that, then said, "Yeah, you right. No police!"

"Of course I'm right. That's why I'm assistant manager and you the taco flipper. Come on, let's get out of here. How's about we unload some of this cash? You hungry?"

"Yeah. Where you like go?"

"McDonald's."

"Right on."

The
Hurricane

For my twelfth birthday my mother got me a pair of ten-pound dumbbells and a booklet that showed how you could build your arms and chest big enough to beat up anyone who kicked sand in your face at the beach. And it only took *six* weeks.

Ho! I liked that!

You couldn't tear me away from those dumbbells.

I worked like a dog before and after school and sometimes put in a few hours on the weekends. Soon I actually began to feel the muscles in my arms and chest getting bigger. I was becoming invincible, though I wasn't so sure I wanted to get in any fights at the beach.

But I did wonder about something: How come Mom got me the dumbbells? I'd never asked for them. In fact, I never once in my life even thought I needed bigger muscles. So why'd she buy them?

When I brought it up, she said, "Gee, I don't know, Joey. It's what your father would have gotten you . . . isn't it?"

I shrugged.

Who knows?

My father was a big fat blank spot. He and my mom split up before I was even born. I met him once when he came back to visit the islands. I liked him. He was nice to me. He was Mom's height and was dressed in shorts, T-shirt, and rubber slippers, like everybody else. But now he lived in Las Vegas with his new wife, Marissa. That's about it.

I had a stepfather, too, for about a year and a half. But he was killed by his best friend in a hunting accident. Now I live with Mom, Darci, my seven-year-old sister from my stepdad, and Stella, our teenage live-in babysitter. Me, in a house of girls.

So you could say my luck with dads wasn't very good. The dumbbells were about that, I guessed—Mom trying to be a dad, too.

One night she came into my room. It was late, maybe nine o'clock, since she doesn't even get home from work until around seven. She picked up one of the dumbbells, then sat down on my bed and started curling it. "Got your homework done?"

"Almost," I said, but I hadn't even thought about it yet.

"Things okay at school?"

"Yeah, sure."

Mom nodded. "Good. You know, I bet Ledward can show you how to use these things."

"Pshh," I snickered. What did Ledward know? He was a tour bus driver, not a weight lifter. He was also Mom's twenty-six-year-old boyfriend. She was thirty-one.

Ledward was an okay guy. I liked him. He was Hawaiian-Chinese and big as a house. But I didn't want him or anyone else to know I was working on my muscles.

"I'll ask him," Mom said.

"What?"

"Ledward. I'll ask him to show you how to use these weights."

"Mom, all you do is lift them."

"He'll know, you'll see."

She put down the dumbbell and picked up my football, then tossed it up and down, kind of clumsily. What's going on? I wondered. Why's she here?

"Hey, let's go toss the ball around," she said. "What say?"

I glanced out the window. It was pitch-black.

"Okay," I said.

Outside, vague light glowed from the house, enough to throw a ball around. The toads were croaking down by the canal that ran past our house at the bottom of our sloped, grassy yard. I stepped lightly because sometimes they came up into the yard and dug down into the grass and hid there, and I didn't like stepping on their bloated bodies.

"I thought I told you to mow the lawn today," Mom said. But she didn't sound mad.

"I . . . I didn't have time."

Mom nodded. "Listen to me, Joey. It's very important that you cut the grass first thing after school tomorrow, okay? Will you do that for me?"

"First thing?"

"Before I get home. It's Friday, and I want the place to look nice for Ledward."

"All right."

"Thank you. Here. Catch."

She quickstepped back and tried to throw the ball like a quarterback on TV. It wobbled out and fell short. "Sorry."

I jogged up and got it, then tossed it back.

We were only about twenty paces apart, and still she couldn't make it. She was small, only a hair taller than me. I moved closer.

She tried again. This time the ball made it to me.

"You got a good arm," I said.

We did that a few more times.

It was fun. We hardly ever did anything together. I didn't know why she was doing this, but I wasn't about to ask and ruin it.

Mom stopped throwing and started to cry. "What's wrong?" I said, walking over. "Did I do something?"

She wiped her eyes with the back of her hand. "No . . . no . . . I just love you so much," she said. "But I can't even throw a ball with you."

She tried to smile.

"What do you mean? You were just throwing it."

"Am I a good mother, Joey?"

"A good mother?"

She put her hand on my cheek.

She hugged me.

Then handed me the ball and went into the house.

Back in my room I climbed the ladder to the top bunk and lay on my stomach, propped up on my elbows. I had stuff to read for school: three pages. That was all. What a joke. I'd read a paragraph, then drift into some thought. Like why was Mom being so weird?

I jumped when a sudden breeze rustled the bushes outside.

Jeez! I was getting spooked in my own room, if you could call that place I lived in a room. What it was was half the garage. One flimsy wood wall stood between my bunk bed and Mom's beat-up old car. On the ceiling was a single bulb in a circular, cake-shaped fixture with a few small moths glued to it. On one side of the light, a model B-52 hung by a piece of thread with its nose pointing down.

I tried to read.

The gulf which separated the chiefs, or alii, *and the commoners had to be accepted. No one dared question the fact that chiefs were descendants of the gods.*

Another short gust of wind rustled the bushes. I looked up. The weather must be changing.

I stuck my pencil in my mouth and bit down, crunching into the yellow paint—then spat the pencil out.

A centipede was oozing out of the rock-and-cement wall along the opposite side of my room. There were cracks in the mortar where those things came out of at night when the place was quiet.

Icy prickles rose up all over my neck.

The centipede was red brown, with dark bands dividing its segments. It undulated on a hundred spiky legs, flowing and rippling down the rock, following the rough contour like a snake. It had to be five inches long at least.

I felt sick to my stomach.

A countertop ran along that side of my room, and the centipede flowed down onto it and scurried behind a picture of my grampa in a standing frame.

I spat bits of yellow pencil paint off my tongue, waiting for the centipede to come back out.

I froze, afraid to even move.

Centipedes stung, they were ugly, and I hated them more than scorpions and wasps and blue-bubble Portuguese man-of-wars. I even hated them more than black widows, which hid in girls' hair at school and could kill you, a true fact I'd heard from a kid on my street named Frankie. But worse than all that, centipedes made me sick because of one time when I was with Willy and Julio and went to get a drink of water, hanging my head under the faucet on the side of our house, and a *monster* centipede came scrambling out into my mouth.

Ghhaaaaaaaaahh! I ran around in circles, spitting and gagging and wiping my tongue off with my hand. The centipede disappeared into the grass. Willy and Julio thought it was the funniest thing they'd ever seen.

Now I turned my book over and inched down the ladder, keeping my eyes on that picture frame. I slipped out into the garage, then into the house.

Everything was dark and quiet.

My feet were silent on the cool linoleum kitchen floor, on the scratchy grass mats in the living room, on the waxed concrete hallway down toward my mother's darkened bedroom.

At first I thought everyone was asleep.

But as I passed by Stella's room, I saw a sliver of light running along the bottom of her closed door. I could hear her radio, too, playing low. I tiptoed by. If she knew I was scared of a centipede, she'd torment me for weeks with her smirks.

Stella was seventeen years old. She was from Biloxi, Mississippi, a place she said was a lot like Hawaii. She came out here to live with her aunt. But that didn't work out, so she looked around for a live-in baby-sitting job. She was a junior at Kailua High School and didn't want to leave her friends.

Mom slept curled up on her side, facing the wall. I crept closer, tripping over her fat scrapbook, where she kept magazine cutouts of her future dream house.

"Mom," I whispered.

She bolted up. "Huh? Oh . . . Joey. You startled me."

"There's a centipede in my room."

Mom sighed and lay back down. "It'll go away. Go back to bed."

I waited a moment, then said, "I can't sleep with it in there."

Mom reached down to the floor, fumbling with her eyes shut. "Here, take my slipper and kill it."

I took it. A flimsy rubber thong.

Mom rolled back over to face the wall.

"Good night, Joey."

Back in my room I reached out with the slipper and knocked the frame over. The centipede woke up and raced across the counter with me slapping after it.

Whop! Missed.

Whop! Missed.

Whop!

I was too afraid to get close enough to actually hit it.

It ran behind my U.S. Army ammo box.

Whop! Whop!

The ammo box jumped, and the loose machine-gun shells inside it rattled. I hit my U.S. Army helmet liner and sent it flying to the floor with a loud, thwacking crash.

Whop!

The centipede slipped down a crack in the back of the counter, then went under the counter.

I stepped back, my heart pounding.

I dropped the slipper and lunged back up the ladder. I checked under my sheets for more centipedes, looked under my book, under my pillow and in the pillowcase, then sat there with my heart trying to leap up out of my throat.

After a few minutes I picked up my book.

The gulf which separated the chiefs . . .

The next day after school a huge mass of clouds swarmed in from the west and swallowed the islands. The whole sky rolled toward the earth and coiled down around the mountaintops. Shaggy beards of rain hung deep into the valleys, turning everything gray.

Me, Willy, and Julio were out in the middle of our street. My hair stood straight up from all the electricity in the air. A gust of wind whipped up and flapped my shirt. A miniature tornado twirled in the dust along the side of the road, and cool earth smells of mud and iron rose from the ground.

Just up the street Maya came bounding out of her house, and when she saw us she waved and shouted, *"Bring it on!"*

There wasn't one of us who didn't love a good storm.

Except Stella.

"Look at her," I said, glancing back at her looking out of our plate-glass living room window.

"How come she don't come out?" Julio said.

"She's worried. She thinks a hurricane is coming."

Willy raised his eyebrows. "Sounds good to me."

"Come out!" I shouted, knowing she'd rather be in a room full of furry spiders than in a hurricane. But this was no hurricane . . . yet.

Stella ran her finger across her throat, meaning she was going to get me for making fun of her.

I laughed.

In a way I couldn't blame her for being scared. She'd been in some bad hurricanes. She told me she once saw a stop sign stabbed halfway through a pine tree by the force of the wind. She told me about the ruins of houses along the oceanfront in Biloxi and Gulfport, most of them little more than tangled piles of sticks.

"You have no idea what you're even talking about," she said when I told her storms were fun. "You're just a stupid little boy and you always will be. Unless, of course, something wakes you up. Which would be a miracle."

"We've had hurricanes here, too," I said. "And I didn't see any of that. You're just trying to scare me."

She smirked. "Someday you're going to regret that you were born with such a small brain. You just wait, buddy."

Buddy.

She liked that word.

I turned back to Willy and Julio. "Anyways, what's she so scared of? This ain't even a hurricane. It's just a regular old storm."

Later I was sitting on the grass with Darci where our yard started to slope down to the canal. I glanced over my shoulder when I heard a car pull up.

Ledward spilled out of his canvas-topped Jeep and hitched up his pants, all dressed up for Mom. He wore a yellow-and-green Hawaiian shirt, hanging loose, Hawaiian-style. He even had on shoes.

He saw me and lifted his chin, Hello, then walked over. He was so tall it hurt my neck just to look up at him. Darci leaned into me. Even though

Ledward had been coming around for about six months now, his size still scared her.

"Hey," I said.

"What you two looking at out there?" he said.

I shrugged. "Nothing."

He looked up, scanned the sky. "Storm coming."

"You heard if it's going to be big?" I said.

"No. But pro'bly. Yeah, I t'ink prob'ly."

I nodded, hoping he was right.

"You mine if I wait for your mama?"

"Sit," I said.

He eased down and sat facing the canal with his arms resting on his propped-up knees. He peeked around me. "Hi, Darcigirl."

Darci moved back so he couldn't see her.

Ledward chuckled.

We sat a moment, saying nothing.

Then Ledward said, "We going Buzz Steak House tonight, me and Angela." That's my mom, Angela.

I nodded. "I like that place."

A bufo croaked down in the weeds by the water.

"Grass getting kine of long," Ledward said.

Dang. I'd forgotten all about the grass. But Mom wasn't home yet. I could still do it, I guess. "Angela told me you had one centipede in your room."

"Yeah," I said. Man, was there anyone she didn't tell stuff to?

"Still in there?"

I nodded.

"You got to cut 'um up, you know."

"Huh?"

"Chop 'um into lot of small pieces. If you just cut 'um one time, no good. The t'ing come back as two."

Darci peeked around me at Ledward, but he was staring off over the canal.

"What do you mean, come back?"

"If you make two chops, then what you got is t'ree of them. Still alive, ah?"

"For real? You're not making this up?"

"But if you make more chops, then you got 'um."

Was he joking?

He turned to look at me, kind of half-grinning. Darci moved back out of sight. The look on Ledward's face said *You better listen up.*

"It could really grow into three centipedes?" I said.

"Sure. Hard to kill those buggahs."

That night the wind grew stronger.

Mom and Ledward went out to Buzz's, leaving me home with Stella and Darci. But I stayed out in my room.

I sat on the bottom bunk curling my dumb-bells, with my heavy U.S. Army jungle knife lying next to me. I was thinking about what Ledward said about chopping up the centipede, how it could come back as more of them if you weren't careful. The knife was gruesome, almost as big as a machete. You could probably kill an alligator with it. I was thinking maybe it might be too clumsy to cut up a centipede, with all the parts running away in every direction. But the thought of going after it with something smaller made me cringe.

Sooner or later I'd have to deal with it.

I put down the dumbbells.

With the knife in one hand, I got up and peeked behind the frame, then checked the back edge of the counter, and the rock wall.

Nothing.

I got up on the counter and peeked into the dark crack where I'd seen it flowing out and down with its hundred shivering legs.

Still nothing.

I found a paper clip and bent it straight. But I couldn't stick it in the crack. If the centipede was in there, and I disturbed it, it would come out lightning fast.

Maybe it had gone back outside.

And maybe not.

I climbed up to the top bunk, taking the knife with me, then reached down and shut off the light with the point of the blade.

I fell asleep listening to the sound of the wind

knocking at my bedroom windows, the screens
rattling in their frames.

A while later the wind woke me up, a constant gust singing through the swamp grass and the
ironwood trees out by the golf course that edged
our street. I could see no lights outside my window.

I got up and put my face up to the screen.

Ledward's Jeep was back.

I tried the light switch. It didn't work.

The storm was growing, getting bigger and better by the hour. I lay back with my hands behind
my head, listening to the sounds and dreaming of
daybreak, when I could go out and roam the
streets with my friends.

A few minutes later I heard Ledward start up
his Jeep, then drive off.

Sometime past midnight the rains came. The
downpour was deep, full, and heavy, pummeling
the earth. By morning dangerous floodwaters
would be raging down from the hills, sloshing past
my house in the muddy brown canal.

Just after dawn I was jarred awake by an explosion of thunder rumbling across the sky.
Massive boulders—settling.

I threw off my sheet and leaped down from my
bunk. Looking out my bedroom window, I could

barely see the canal. Everything was smudged by a silvery rain that now fell slanted in the wind. I could make out the golf-course bridge that crossed the canal, or the faint line of it anyway. But beyond that everything was a blur.

"Yes!" I whispered.

I tried my radio.

The power was back.

I whirled the dial. The storm was for real, all right. And the radio said it was only the beginning. A powerful disturbance was bearing down on the islands from the west. It was going to be a big one, so tie everything down.

Just before noon lightning began flashing through the cracks in the clouds. Then more thunder, so loud and so close it shook the house. Stella and Darci stood next to me at the big plate-glass window watching the storm swallow the island.

The canal was now white with raindrops exploding on its surface, the water level rising fast, bulging seaward, climbing the slope of our yard.

I was itchy to get outside, to run down and get Willy, and roam around in the storm. But first I wanted the lightning to stop.

"You kids get away from that window," Mom said. "What if thunder blows it apart and it shatters all over your faces?"

We stood back. Could thunder really do that?

When Mom left the room, I crept back to the window.

Minutes later Ledward drove up in his Jeep,

headlights on, wipers slapping on high speed. I could barely see him through the windshield. He parked as close as he could get, then got out and ducked into the garage.

I ran into the kitchen, where he would come into the house, Darci at my heels.

Ledward flung open the door, cursing the weather.

Darci ran back out to the living room.

"What are you *doing* here?" Mom said.

Ledward shook the rainwater off his arms, then grabbed a dirty dish towel and wiped his face with it. "I wanted to make sure you all right."

"Oh, that's so sweet," Mom said, which Ledward brushed off with a frown.

His T-shirt clung to his body. He couldn't have been in the rain for more than three seconds, but he looked as if he'd just climbed out of a swimming pool. "Watch the canal," he said. "It could flood."

A two-inch roach scurried across the kitchen floor. Mom took her rubber slipper off and whacked it before it went under the refrigerator. White guts oozed out along its sides. Mom got a napkin and wiped it up.

"The rain drive 'um in," Ledward said.

No kidding, I thought. Bugs run this place.

"Drives in the centipedes, too," Mom said. "Isn't that right, Joey?"

Ledward turned to me. "You cut that t'ing up yet?"

I shook my head.

"How come? Scared of it?"

"No."

"Come. I help you," Ledward said.

"Right now?"

"This minit."

Mom and I followed him out to my room. He noticed my combat knife and picked it up.

"I hate that thing," Mom said.

Ledward turned it over, felt the weight of it in his hand, set it back down. Then he took a small bone-handled pocketknife from his shorts and opened it. "So where is it?"

"I . . . I don't know." I pointed to the dark space below the counter. "Probably under there somewhere."

Ledward squatted down and looked around.

I stepped back, expecting the centipede to come racing out like before. Ledward duckwalked beside the counter, looking up under it. Then he grunted and sat back on his heels.

He grinned. "Look."

I squatted down. There it was, sleeping on the rock wall. When Ledward touched it with the knife, it shot away, snaking up the wall at lightning speed, slithering through the crack behind the counter.

I stumbled back, falling into Mom, who banged against the door.

Ledward stood.

He peeked over the mess on my counter,

looking for the centipede's hiding place. Slowly he moved a stack of books aside, the pocketknife ready.

The centipede raced out into the open.

Tick!

He cut it into two writhing pieces.

Tick! Tick!

Four segments, curling, flipping, legs clawing air.

Ledward wiped the blade on his shorts and folded it back into the handle. "No boddah you now," he said.

"Let's go make some hot chocolate," Mom said, sighing.

Ledward winked and tapped my shoulder, then followed Mom into the kitchen, leaving me gaping at the centipede parts. What was I supposed to do now?

A few minutes later Stella poked her head in my door.

"What do *you* want?" I said.

"Oh, nothing. I just wanted to see what you had Ledward do for you."

I stepped between her and the centipede parts.

She grinned. "I just love watching you squirm."

"I'm not squirming."

"Oh?" Stella glanced behind her, then looked back and whispered, "Well, listen . . . how mad do you think that thing's *mate* is gonna be?" She winked and backed away. "Bye, little buddy."

Stella, the thorn in my foot.

I went back into the kitchen to tell Mom I was going over to Willy's house. Stella was poking around in the fridge for something to eat. She ignored me.

Darci was back, sitting at the table with a bowl of Rice Krispies and reading my Classic Comic of *Tom Sawyer* with milk dripping off her chin onto the pages. "Hey, don't get milk on the pages, okay?"

"I'm not," she said, wiping the comic with her elbow.

"Where's Mom?" I said.

"Looking out the window."

Maybe I should just go, I thought. She might say no.

"Can I have it?" Darci said.

"What?"

She picked up the comic.

"Yeah, sure, it's all warped with milk, anyway."

I went into the living room. Mom and Ledward stood at the plate-glass window watching the wind and rain.

"I'm going over to Willy's house," I told Mom.

She looked at Ledward. "What do you think?"

Ledward shrugged.

Mom glanced back out the window. "Well, you stay inside when you get there, understand? Don't go wandering around in this wind. And stay away from the canal. Don't go near it, you hear me?"

"Yeah," I said, then bolted out to my room.

I put on some jeans and rolled them up to just

below my knees. Then I put on a sweatshirt and a hooded army-surplus rain poncho that was three times too big for me.

Outside, the rain whapped down. The wind plastered the hood to one side of my face. I turned and walked with the wind hammering into my back as I staggered up the street toward Willy's house. The road was warm under my bare feet. The rain was warm, too. I could have stayed out there all day, letting the storm shove me every which away.

I thumped on Willy's door. His mom answered.

"My God, Joey, what are you doing out on a day like this?"

"Is Willy home?"

"Of course he's home. Go around and come in through the garage. Leave that wet poncho out there."

"Heyyy," Willy said when I poked my head into his room. He was playing with his lead soldiers. Battalions all lined up, two armies facing each other. He shot a man down with a rubber band, his long straight hair hanging into his eyes.

"You want to go down to the beach?" I said. "Check out the ocean?"

"I'll get my poncho."

It was exactly like mine. We'd gotten them together from an army-surplus store in Honolulu. "Mom!" Willy shouted from the garage. "I'm going over to Joey's house!"

"It's too stormy," she said.

We left anyway.

We cut through Willy's backyard and climbed the fence and fought the wind down the street to Kalapawai Market, where we bought Fudgsicles to eat in the storm. We were the only customers. In fact, we were the *last* customers. "I'm closing up," the lady said. "Too dangerous outside. You boys go home."

"We're going there now," I said, peeling the paper from my Fudgsicle.

"Good. You be smart boys, now."

We walked out and headed for the beach.

The sand was gone, covered now with a wild, frothy-white ocean that churned and boiled its way up over the beach and into people's yards. I was glad we had ponchos, because the rain stung and the wind shredded palm fronds and tore olive-sized pinecones off the ironwood trees and machine-gunned them past our heads.

I faced into the wind and opened my mouth. It blew my hood off and popped out my cheeks. I threw my Fudgsicle stick toward the sea, and it blew it back over my shoulder. Willy couldn't make his go forward, either.

"Let's check the canal!" Willy shouted, his poncho snapping in the wind. He gripped it under his chin to keep the hood on his head.

I yelled back, but the wind ripped the words right out of my mouth.

We lurched over to a grove of trees that overlooked the canal. On a regular day it bogged up there. But today the water was alive and pulsing toward the sea in fat, muddy gulps.

The wind nearly knocked me over. I had to spread my feet apart to stand my ground. I got this urge to go down to the edge of the water and feel its power as it raced to the sea.

I glanced at Willy, then inched down the slope, grabbing ironwood roots where they were exposed in the bank. Clumps of wet sand broke away under my feet and slid down and were immediately eaten by the fast-moving water.

"What are you doing?" Willy shouted, his voice flying away in the wind.

"Going down to the water!"

"Why?"

I didn't answer. Too hard.

I studied the swirling mud-water gushing below me. It didn't look so bad. I inched closer, so close now I could stick my foot in. I waded out a step, then another. Up to my knees. The heavy water tugged at my shins. I dug into the sand as it fell away beneath my feet.

I looked up at Willy and yelled, *"Yeee-haaa!"*

Willy grinned and started down the slope.

Foop!

The angry water ripped my feet out from under me and took me down.

And under.

The poncho clamped around me, blinded me. Pinned my arms back. I came up, went under, came up again, gasping as I sailed toward the sea.

I tried to swim, but my arms were tangled in the poncho. My sweatshirt sucked up water like a sponge. I caught a glimpse of Willy stumbling down the slope, then racing along the shore parallel to me. I went under again. Gritty water scraped my eyeballs.

Gagging. Choking.

Horror slammed me. I was going to die.

The current spit me closer to shore. I dug my toes into the sand, trying to stop. But the force of the river was fierce.

Willy sprinted along the beach, hood off, poncho flapping. I tried to yell but could only gag and spit. I struggled to free my arms.

My feet slowed me some, but I couldn't get close enough to shore. I sailed out and out, racing toward the frenzied sea.

Willy yelled something.

I managed to work my right arm out from under the poncho and claw my way toward him, now almost into the throat of the canal, where the riptide screamed into the ocean.

Willy stepped into the water and reached out and grabbed my hand, his eyes bulging. He pulled too quickly, and our hands slipped apart. I clawed air, trying to get back to him. Willy reached and reached, stumbling ahead. He fell to his knees and caught my hand. I swung in an arc to shallower water, my suffocating poncho dragging me under.

But Willy held on and pulled me out.

The two of us staggered up and stumbled away

from the canal, tripping and falling. I started gagging, then crying.

We sprawled in the sand up near the trees, the wind howling in my ears, snapping through my tangled, sand-caked hair. I was shivering so hard I could hardly breathe, rocking and weeping silently.

"*You okay?*" Willy shouted, even though he was right next to me.

I nodded.

My throat stung from swallowed mud and sand. I could feel the scratch of silt trapped under my eyelids.

"*Let's get out of here!*" Willy said, pulling me up.

We split up when we got near our street. I didn't say a word to him, not even thanks for saving my life.

I staggered home, burst into my room, and ripped off the poncho with trembling hands. I threw my clammy jeans and sweatshirt in a wet lump on the floor by my dumbbells, then wrapped myself in my blanket and sat on the lower bunk, still shaking, staring with blank and burning eyes at a swarm of ants already hauling off the rotting centipede parts.

Later that day I skulked around the house. Mom didn't seem to see the fine grains of sand that were stuck to my scalp. I don't think she even

noticed how quiet I'd become or caught the shock
I saw in my red-veined eyes every time I looked in
the mirror.

But Stella did, studying me as if she knew
something had happened but wasn't sure what.

I sat apart from everyone, out on the lanai under the overhang, watching the trees sway in the
jungle beyond our backyard.

Mom came out and sat next to me in a sagging
white-and-yellow vinyl chair. For a while we didn't
speak or even look at each other.

Finally Mom said, "Will this weather ever end?"

I shrugged.

My brain was numb, and Mom seemed a thousand miles away.

"Joey . . ."

I waited, staring at fat raindrops bouncing in
the giant mud puddle under Darci's swing set.

I turned when Mom didn't go on.

"Do you . . . do you see any wrinkles around
my eyes? I mean, have you noticed any?"

"Wrinkles?"

"Or gray hair, have you noticed any of those?
Because I found one last week."

She paused. "Am I getting old?"

I studied her profile, lingering on her smooth,
perfect face, her long hair tucked back over her
ear on one side, falling like golden brown silk on
the other. She hardly looked out of high school.
"You're not old, Mom," I whispered.

We sat watching the rain, saying nothing. I wondered what Willy was doing. I was feeling kind of embarrassed now for what had happened.

I jumped when Mom spoke again.

"Are you sure I'm a good mother?"

"What?"

"Because I'm trying, Joey."

"I know, Mom."

"I'm really trying."

Annakua

Kailua-Kona, Hawaii.

Massive black sky. A zillion pin-prick stars sweep up and over the island. The moon is five hours gone and the morning birds have yet to gather.

Seventy-six degrees and no breeze. Not a whisper.

Jimmy Smith and Rats Aoki, both seventeen, wait in the early-morning darkness for a truck to take them to the pier. They sit on the rocks along the old coast road, a dark and peaceful sea lapping at their feet.

But for the whispering water, it is dead silent. No cars have come or gone since they walked there from their dusty homes just inland. Its the third week of their summer job.

They talk quietly.

Hey, Jimmy. You like hear one awesome story?

About what?

Okay. Had one boat, ah? Sampan. Was *loaded.*

Wait wait wait. This a story or is it true?

True. My uncle told me um when he came our house last night.

Oh. Okay go on.

Like I said, had this boat and was *loaded.*

With what?

Tst, I getting to that. Shuddup . . . Okay . . . Was coming home from five, six days fishing out past Kauai. They was bringing back *ahi,* yeah? Hundred, hundred-fifty-pound kind. *Ahi,* the yellowfin tuna.

I know whats *ahi.* Whose boat?

I dont know. One guy, thats all. Anyways, there they was, loaded. The boat way down in the water, couple feet from the rail, ah? And it was rocking and rolling and hoo those guys on that boat was coming nervous, specially when they see the straight clouds coming in the sky. You know, straight from the wind, yeah? Sign of bad weather.

Yeah yeah, bad weather.

Not getting bad by the boat yet but coming bad outside by the horizon. Can you see it?

What?

Can you *see* it?

See what?

The straight clouds, the bad weather, the . . . Why I even try talk to you I dont know.

Come on, Rats. Tell the story. Tell it.

Tst. Just try to see what I saying, ah? Aint that hard. Okay, was fifteen guys on that boat, twelve Asian guys—new guys from Vietnam or Korea or Laos, I dont know, someplace like that. But anyways, also had two Hawaiian guys and one bossman who was the skippah. Local guy. Maybe Japanee. Anyways was his boat. The rest of them just working for him.

You just making the bossman Japanee because you Japanee, yeah, Rats?

Jimmy, I going slap your head you dont shut it up.

Kay-okay, just joking for crying out loud.

Maybe I aint going tell you this. Stupit haole.

I was *joking* I said.

> Jimmy waits, but Rats just sits there. Out on the ocean a small yellow light bobs in and out of view. Night fisherman. Jimmy spits.

I know why they call you Rats. When you was born and you came out and your mama saw your dingaling, she said, *Rats!* I was hoping for one girl.

Thats good, Jimmy. You made that up all by yourself?

Yeah cool yeah? Okay, so this loaded sampan was coming home. All the holds was full with *ahi* and pretty soon the wind was picking up and the ocean was coming rough and had swells coming from the side and was making that boat rock and roll and those guys was getting nervous. Then what?

Okay if you going shut it up I tell you um. You going shuddup?

Yeah yeah, what happened?

Okay. One of the Hawaiian guys, he went up to the skippah and tell, "Skippah you gotta dump some fish. Look the clouds. Going get bad. We too heavy. We could capsize."

He said that to the skippah?

True. And the skippah look at him and tell back, "I da skippah on dis boat and if you tink I going dump couple tousand bucks of fish you crazy and also if we did need dump um den I make dat decision not you."

Whoa, and then what the Hawaiian guy said?

Nothing. What he can say? Aint his boat, yeah? So he just went back and got more nervous with the rest of the guys who was all watching the clouds and the swells and smelling the wind. *Ho man,* they thinking. The Hawaiian guy, he looking for land, yeah? But no can see nothing. Then little bit later one guy saw um. Small blue mountaintop coming out from the sea. Was Kauai, ah? Way off. Probly about fifteen miles.

Yahh! That far and the storm was coming.

And the storm was coming.

Ho! And the skippah said he aint dumping no fish.

Uh-huh, and the guys waiting around and the
wind picking up and the boat rolling more worse
and by now they nervous as rats, so the Hawaiian
guy go back to the skippah. Tell, "You gotta dump
some fish, man. We going *capsize!*" And the skippah tell the guy he going get arrested for mutiny if
he dont shut up.

Mutiny? He can do that?

I dont know. Anyways thats what my uncle told us
thats what he said. So listen, now all those guys
thinking, man man *man!* The Asian guys really
soaking their pants now because most of them no
can swim, yeah? And the sky turning, coming dark,
and could smell the storm in the air. You know
how you can do that, smell um? But the one thing
is they can see Kauai. Pretty soon they see um little
bit more, little bit more. They going closer, ah?
Now most of the island stay up out of the ocean so
at least they had that, the land. At least they could
see land.

Yeah but they still way out.

Who telling this, you or me?

You telling it, Rats. You da man. Go on.

You making me mad you know?

How come you so jumpy today? You had one fight with Janelle last night or what?

How you knew that?

I didnt.

Then why you said it?

I dont know. Cuz you so pissy?

Stupit haole.

Hey.

> Rats throws a stone into the sea.
> A rooster crows, somewhere way off.
> Over the mountain behind them the sky begins to lighten.

You like hear the rest of it or what?

Sure. Go ahead. All the guys was scared.

Yeah and so now the ocean coming *intense,* yeah? All those Asian guys get *mempachi* eyes, all puff out like bubblefish. They scared that boat going flip. And of course the Hawaiian guys worried too because they *know* there going be trouble because now the swells was coming from the side and getting more big and more big and now even the *skippah* was getting nervous. But still he aint going dump no fish. He like the money, ah? But he bring the boat around so the bow going into the swells. Forget trying to make land. Now he thinking he going ride um out, let the storm pass. The bow going up the swell and down the behind side until the next one take um up again. But the thing is . . .

The next ones stay coming more close now.

Yeah they coming more close, *boom, boom,* one after the other, and that bow going higher each time it climb because of the swells getting bigger.

What about Kauai? Could they still see that?

Yeah probly but now had clouds coming all over the sky. Getting hard for see and all those poor buggahs was hanging on to whatever they could find on that boat to hang on to. Up and down and up and down. Pretty soon they going up up up way up, then *ka-boom,* down the other side. *Boom! Bam! Slam!* A *nightmare.*

Man I glad I wasnt on that boat.

You dont know how glad you going be till I tell you the rest of it, Jimmy.

This one great *story* man. You really think its true?

Sure its true. My uncle aint no liar. So that sampan going up then down then up then down till finally one last time that boat come down and *foomp!* Never come back up.

Yai-yah!

The bow went sink in the next swell. Went *under* the swell, *under* um. When it come back up . . . the boat was capsize.

Ohhh God. Upside down?

Of course upside down. What you think capsize means?

So the guys was where? In the water?

No, they was home in bed watching TV, you stupit haole. Of course they was in the water. So now had all these guys trying to swim and trying for grab on the boat, and the hull of the sampan stay looking up and was all green and slippery and nobody could climb on top um. So you know what those guys did? *Uku* smart, them. They took off their belts and put um together two by two and threw um over the keel and one guy got on one side and another guy got on the other side and they pulled themselves up like that till they was sitting on the hull or hanging on it by their belts.

Jeese!

And they was *fif—teen* miles from land.

Thats a long swim.

Yeah but they no can swim, yeah? Even the skippah. But that aint the worst of it.

No?

No. The worst of it was all that fish in the hold. Now that the boat was upside down all those hundreds of fat bloody smelly dead tuna was now falling slow motion out of those holds and spreading out in the sea . . . under the boat. Slow and slow, drifting down . . . down. Can you see it?

Yahh. I don't think I want to hear any more of this.

You guessed it. Sharks. Oceanic white tips. Came like wolfs. Travel in a pack, yeah? Attack and eat anything they see. They dont care what it is—fish, cane trash, coconut, soda pop can, even one truck engine if was down there. Anyways Uncle said had twenty, thirty, something like that. Was me, I would be pass out just to see those fins swirling around making whirlpool water. Even now I can

feel my legs in that ocean and I wasnt even there.
Aaahh. *Creepy.*

I dont want to hear it.

> Silence.
> Waves lapping.
> A dog barks. One, two arfs.
> Headlights down the road, somebody slow-
> driving toward them. Rats looks that way.
> But not Jimmy.

So what? The sharks ate those guys?

I thought you said you didnt want to hear no more.

Yeah but you cant stop now, Rats.

> The headlights are now nearly upon them.
> The driver takes his foot off the gas, and when
> he does, the headlights dim.
> Brakes squeak, slowing. Their ride.

> Jimmy and Rats stand and brush off the backs of
> their shorts, and the truck stops in the middle of
> the road. Two other boys are in the back, Willy
> Mombouguette and Felix Kalama, both a year
> younger than Jimmy and Rats. Rats stretches,
> yawns loudly.

> The driver, a man they call Boss, leans out.

Whachoo waiting for? Breakfast? Get in the truck, arready!

Rats and Jimmy climb over the tailgate.

Willy and Felix reach out to slap hands with Jimmy and Rats. Rats grins.

Whasamatta? You look tired. Too early for you small kids? Still like sleep?

Rats settles down with his back to the cab.
Willy and Felix look at him. Jimmy elbows Rats.

So, what? The sharks ate those guys or what?

Okay where was I. Yeah. The sharks. Well they didnt care about those guys, oh no, not when they got all that Christmas falling out of that boat. Can you imagine? What a *feast*. Those white tips start scarfing um down, blood making the ocean come brown, whirlpools, whitewater, fins, and bloody meat and man that place was a *feeding* frenzy.

Willy and Felix wake up now.
Rats looks right in their faces and says again, *feeding frenzy,* and their eyebrows pop up.
Jimmy shudders.

Man, Rats, make my skin crawl just to *think* about it.

Must have been a *night*mare.

No kidding, brah. Those Asian guys was fresh out of piss. But not those Hawaiian guys, not them. They was thinking, when those sharks *pau* all that free food, then they going come get us and they not going stop until every last bite of us is gone.

Yeah but wasnt everybody up on the hull? Out of the water?

Sure but still had rough ocean, yeah? The hull was rising and falling and rolling just like before, but now was upside down remembah. Those guys was out of the water one minute then under it the next, hanging on by those belts.

God.

God wasnt there that day. Oh no. So the two Hawaiian guys know one thing is for sure: they aint going live if they stay like that. So you know what they did? They left the boat.

What?

They told the skippah they going swim to Kauai for get help.

Not. You couldnt swim through those sharks.

Yeah but those Hawaiians knew something. You
see, they went check the water, look at those
sharks, see what they can see and what they
saw was one shark wasnt eating, was just cruis-
ing around by the hull, his eye looking up at
them.

Whoa. *Spooky*.

The two guys watch that shark, watch it and watch
it, and finally one guy nod his head. Yeah, he said,
yeah. He recognize um, yeah? Was his aumakua,
come to help him. He recognize that shark by the
markings.

What you mean? He recognize the shark?

Was his family protector. His relation. Hawaiians
got that, you know, spirit protectors. Some are
lizards, some are owls, eels, dogs. And some are
sharks. And this guys one was shark, and man was
he relieved to see it.

Nah. You believe in that superstition?

Are you kidding? Of course I believe in it. You
never heard shark aumakua stories before? You
never heard about the one live at Pearl Harbor?

No.

Thats cuz you haole, why you dont believe it. But whether you do or dont its true. So anyways, what they did was they know those bad sharks stay busy now, eating good fish. And they know had that one protector shark to watch over them. So one guy went lie on top the other guys legs in the ocean. Like this. Made it look like they was one big man, or one big thing. Maybe a log or like that. Ten feet long. Then they started to swim through the feeding sharks with that one good shark swimming by them. Slow and slow. Careful not to stir it up, yeah? Not making whitewater. Just moving their arms. Steel nerves I tell you. Guts.

Nuts you mean.

No. Not nuts. They believed, they believed. So they swam. And lissen to this if you think its superstition: they *made* it. They made it through the pack of wild crazy sharks. And then they broke up and swam. Swam swam swam. All day and all night. Swam all the way to Kauai. And made it.

Ho! Man! I couldnt do that. I would get tired and sink.

Yeah me too probly. But not them. They strong. They made it. But had one problem that good shark could not help them with.

What?

When they got to land they was too damn tired to get up and walk somewheres for help.

Thats a problem all right. For those other guys still hanging on the boat.

But that aint the end of it, Jimmy. Luckily a jeep came, Coast Guard patrol or something. Some kind of military guys, two of them, and they was driving by and when they look down and see two bodies rolling around in the surf down on the beach, they stop and jump out. Run down there thinking had a drowning or a murder, but what they find is those Hawaiian guys. When the Coast Guard guys heard the story they drag the Hawaiians to the jeep and race off to get help for the other guys on the boat.

Willy and Felix are bug-eyed. They watch Rats as the truck cruises through town and drives out onto the pier.

The harbor is still, the water glassy. A single lamp casts a yellowy glow down onto the hull of a fifty-foot sampan tied alongside the pier. *Lady Luck* is painted in black script across its transom.

The boss shuts the truck down and the boys climb out and stand around with their hands in their pockets or tucked under their armpits waiting for the boss to tell them what to do. But the boss walks over to another boat to talk with another fisherman.

So finish the story, Rats. What happened? They went out on a Coast Guard boat and got um?

I feel sorry for you Jimmy, you so slow. If they went on a boat it would be too *late*, it would take too *long*, those sharks eat *fast*. Already it was probly way too late. Think about it. If you able.

But if they didnt have a boat how they going save um?

They didnt.

They didnt even go out?

No they went out. They got in a choppa—rescue choppa—they flew out looking for the sampan. They figure they could drop one rope and pull those guys up inside it. The storm was gone by then and the ocean was smooth as glass. But still it took um a while to find the boat. And when they did . . .

Willy and Felix and Jimmy gape at Rats. Rats walks over to the edge of the pier and spits in the water. The three guys follow him.

Jimmy cant stand it.

What?

Close your eyes.

Close my . . . what for?

Just *close* um.

Tst . . .

Okay. Now see if you can see this. When the choppa got close what they saw was the hull in the water. One shiny-wet hull. Thats all. But then they saw something else, something they never seen before and probly never going see again in their life. *Hey* I said keep your eyes *shut.* Okay imagine this: one after another, again and again, they saw those sharks come up behind that capsize boat and jump out of the water and sail across that hull. Sssssst. Sliding across it, end to end. Ssssssst. All the way. Ssssst, sssssst, like that.

   Nobody says a word.
   Jimmy winces as he imagines what Rats is saying.
   Willy and Felix open their eyes.
   Rats looks at Willy first, then Felix, and he isnt grinning or laughing like it was all a madeup story to scare them.

There wasnt one . . . guy . . . left.

Jimmy opens his eyes.

Thats the worst story I ever heard, Rats. The worst!

Me too, brah. Me too.

Then you *not* lying. Its true. Really went happen.

Thats what I heard.

Tst. Make me like quit this job I tell you. Who wants to go fishing now?

Yeah but was one freak story, yeah, Jimmy? Probly never happen again, not in that way, not like that. So I aint scared of it. But you can bet I going keep myself on top this boat, oh yeah.

You know whats bad, Rats? Those Hawaiian guys. They gotta live with it, with that memory.

Yeah but lucky they Hawaiian.

How you mean?

Hawaiians know their roots. They know the ocean. They know the land. They respect it. And they believe in their aumakua and they dont offend them,

like if they had shark aumakua then they dont eat
shark. Would be like eating your ancestor, yeah? In
the ocean life comes, life goes. They know that.
Just how it is for them. And if they are good they
got help from the spirit world. And anyways I bet a
lot of those guys would rather take their chances
with a shark than a man, specially with guys like
you, Jimmy.

Whatchoo mean guys like me?

Haole.

You got a real problem with haoles, Rats, you
know that? You gotta get over it, man. Just cuz
haole skin is white dont mean we different from
you you know. We just like everybody else.

You are? You just like me? You just like Hawaiians?

Of course.

You could fool me, man.

Why?

Would you swim through sharks like that?

No.

See.

See what? You aint Hawaiian and you wouldnt swim through sharks.

Yes I would, Jimmy.

Tst. Liar.

No. I would swim. I aint going sit around and die from sharks. I would swim, man. I would chance um, try for save myself. Sure I would.

Even if you dont have shark aumakua?

Maybe I do.

Shhh.

Maybe you do, too, Jimmy. Only you too white to believe it.

You think?

Yeah, maybe. You not a bad guy, most of the time. Shhh, the boss coming. Time for go catch fish.

Hey! Dont say that. The fish going hear you then we *never* going catch um. Time for go hunt *pig,* brah. Pig.

Yeah pig. We go hunt pig. Cuz we gotta. We go *chance* um!

Rats and Jimmy tap fists.
Willy and Felix look nervous.
Rats reaches out his fist.

Hows about you, little bruddas? You ready to get
on that boat?

Willy and Felix grin and tap fists with Rats, and
the four boys jump aboard the *Lady Luck*. The
Boss unties the ropes and tosses them on deck,
then jumps on board himself. He pauses a moment and studies the boys standing before him.
He shakes his head, then parts them with a dis-
missing wave of his hand as if they were chickens or goats or cows. He slips behind the wheel
and fires up the diesel and slowly walks the boat
out of the harbor.

The sun is starting to glow behind the mountain
now, and the sky is turning purple blue. Jimmy
is coiling the stern line into a neat pile.

Hey Rats. What finally happened to those
Hawaiian guys?

Nothing. They went back to work. Fishing. Thats
what they do. Shoot, thats what *we* do.

Yeah but it aint what we *want* to do.

We aint rich enough to do what we want to do.

You mean yet.

Yeah yet.

Fifteen minutes later the sun explodes over the mountain. The Boss sits at the wheel, squinting out over the ocean.

Behind him on the stern deck Jimmy, Rats, Willy, and Felix stand facing aft, watching their quiet blue green island slip, slip away.

Frankie Diamond Is Robbing Us Blind

Call us the ShortBoyz.

We're sixth graders in Kailua, island of O'ahu—me, Willy, Rubin, Julio, one girl named Maya Medeiros, and boy, do we need help.

Frankie Diamond is robbing us blind.

And we just got to take it because he's two years older than us and we're all small guys, except for Maya, who's taller than all of us. She's Julio's cousin, too, which is one reason we let her be in the ShortBoyz. But also we let her in because Willy likes her, and then because she has the opposite problem from us: too tall.

Anyway, about Frankie Diamond. He's getting worse.

Last week we were walking home from school. My second-grade sister, Darci, was with us, too, because I have to take care of her in the afternoon until Stella, our live-in sort-of-nanny, gets home from high school. My mom sells jewelry in Honolulu, on the other side of the island, and is gone from seven to seven most of the time.

Anyway, like most days when somebody's got some money, we went to the store after school to buy stuff to eat. Willy and I had eight dollars from mowing the Thompsons' grass, so we bought for everyone.

We each had our own brown paper bag full of things we liked—Hershey's, Butterfinger, *li hing mui,* crackseed, whole plum, cuttlefish, dried shrimp. Mine had two Ball Park mints, one peanut M&M's, one jawbreaker, and a bag of salty-sweet dried shrimp.

We were out in the middle of the big grassy field between Kailua Elementary School and the middle school. Just walking slowly, talking about whatever came up, with the sun boiling down and the cool ocean sitting out there waiting for us.

It was perfect.

Until Frankie Diamond popped out from under the bleachers at the Little League baseball diamond. And slinking out after him were the Andrade brothers, Mike and Tito, who I once saw in the backseat of a police car.

"Aw, man," Willy said.

Frankie saw us and started heading our way with a grin on his face and Mike and Tito flanking him.

We stopped in a clump.

The Andrade brothers glared death our way,

flopping toward us in their too-big camouflage army-fatigue pants, with no shirts and sweat glistening on their shoulders.

Frankie walked tall, grinning.

"Wow," Maya whispered. "I've never seen him this close before. He looks like a movie star."

Willy scowled.

Frankie was even taller than Maya. "Heyyy, liddle men," he said, walking up. "Oh, 'scuse. I see you bugs got couple ladies wit' you today."

Under a black peach-fuzz mustache, the tip of a toothpick peeked out in the corner of his mouth. His face was clean and smooth with no zits, and his eyes were so light you couldn't stop looking at them, the color almost white. One was sleepy, the left one. Looked weird—brown-skin boy with white eyes.

Frankie kept on grinning, standing over us with his muscular arms dangling like eels from his sleeveless white T-shirt. Like always he wore baggy jeans and black U.S. Army dress shoes spit shined to where if you looked down you could see your long, stretched-out face in them.

Hanging off one shoulder was a beat-up black book bag that probably never had a book in it since the day he got it. One time he had a small orange cat in it. Its name was Squeaky and it belonged to Donna Ferris, a girl Frankie liked to tease. Donna didn't think it was funny. Maya told us that.

Anyway, all us guys and Maya lived on the

same street as Frankie. But Frankie was new. He came from Palama district, on Honolulu side. We heard his mom kicked him out and he had to move in with his older brother, Darius, a policeman, who lived with two other cops on our street. Hard to imagine someone like Frankie Diamond living with three cops.

One time me and Willy ran into him by accident. He was sitting cross-legged in front of his house, throwing a pocketknife into the grass. We didn't notice him at first or else we would have cut through somebody's yard.

So I said, "Uh . . . you want to play baseball with us?"

He gave us a long stare with his face pinched up, like he was thinking, Did somebody make a fut?

I should have kept my mouth shut.

So here we were out in the open field with Mike and Tito, the criminal brothers, backing up Frankie Diamond, who was looking down on us with his hands on his hips and that toothpick dancing in his mouth.

A bird flew past, its wings whirring.

Frankie looked up. Then back.

"Whatchoo got in those bags, liddle men?"

All of us tried to sneak our bags behind us, even Darci.

Frankie's grin grew, white teeth gleaming.

"Hey, be nice," he said. "I ain't going bite you. And anyways, even if all you small folks jump on top me one time, I can still kill you, ah? Oh, did you meet my frens?" Frankie grinned without turning toward them.

Mike crossed his arms. Tito stood stone faced, glaring at us. I wondered if Frankie knew just who he'd picked for friends.

"So come on, show me those bags, ah?"

We showed him our bags.

Frankie looked inside every one of them except Darci's, taking out what he wanted, making faces at what he didn't. "Butterfinger? You like that junk?"

From mine he took the dried shrimp and the jawbreaker.

"Aw, man," I said.

Frankie tossed the shrimp to the Andrades and slipped the jawbreaker into his mouth. "It's better to give than to receive," he said, then wagged his eyebrows.

"You got no right, man," Willy said, kind of meekly, avoiding those white eyes.

"Right, wrong . . . no mean not'ing to me, you know what I mean? Little bug?"

When he was done robbing us, we started to walk away.

"Wait a minute, what's your hurry? Hey, you," he said, looking at me. "You live my street, ah? I remember you. What's your name? I forget already. No, wait. Let me guess. Starts with *S*, yeah?"

"It's Joey."

"No, no, no," Frankie said. "Try wait."

He studied me with squinted eyes, his hand on his chin and my jawbreaker bulging in his cheek.

"I got it!" he said, snapping his finger. "Shrimp. Yeah yeah yeah. That's it." He laughed, both eyes closed to slits.

"I said it's Joey."

"Nah, you wrong, brah. I just changed it. From now on you going be Shrimp."

"Shrimp?"

"Like the bag of shrimp you just gave me, ah?"

"Gave you?"

Frankie looked at Maya. "You hear one echo?"

"Echo?" Maya said.

"You folks are freaks, you know that? All of you."

"Freaks?" Willy mumbled.

Frankie's sleepy eye woke up and looked all the way down Willy's throat. The Andrades almost grinned, probably thinking, About time somebody going die.

Willy saw that and quickly stared down into Frankie's spit-shined shoes.

Ho! I thought he was dead.

But Frankie smiled again. "I got an idea. I going give *all* you liddle bugs new names, how's that?"

What could we say?

We stood waiting so we could get it over with and go home. Frankie took his time.

"Yours one going be Shrimp, yeah? I gave you that already."

Fine, I thought.

He moved over and looked down on Willy.

Willy, who's kind of muscular and squatty, kept his gaze on Frankie's throat, which, I noticed, had a silver chain around it. And on the chain was a small cross.

"You going be . . . Mouse," Frankie told Willy, nodding, pleased. He thought we were actually excited to get those names from him, like they were gifts.

"You, what's your name?"

"Julio."

"Julio? You Mexican?"

"No."

"Hmmm. I know. You going be Louse. That's one lice, yeah? You know that?"

Julio nodded.

"Hah! Same-same," Frankie said. "Mouse and Louse." He turned and grinned at the Andrades, who grinned back.

Rubin became Liddlebiddyguy.

I laughed. I couldn't help it. It was funny. Liddlebiddyguy. Rubin glared at me. I tried to stop but it came bursting back up. Like when you can't stop a sneeze.

Frankie towered over Darci. "Whatchoo doing with these ugly bugs, ah? Small kid like you. What you, firs' grade?"

Darci, eyes big as baseballs, stepped behind me.

"She's my sister," I said.

Frankie squatted down, ignoring me.

"Hey," he said softly. "I not going hurt you. Come out from there."

Darci did.

Frankie smiled, face to face with Darci. "What's your name?"

"D-Darci."

He reached out to shake hands. Darci froze up. But Frankie waited patiently, smiling at her. Hesitantly, Darci shook. "Nice to meet you, Darci," he said. "Lissen, anybody ever boddah you, I don't care who it is, you come see Frankie Diamond, okay?"

Darci nodded.

Frankie stood and ruffled her hair. "You going stay Darci. I like that name."

Last was Maya.

Frankie scratched his head, thinking about her. He scratched carefully, though, not wanting to mess up his perfectly greased-back hair.

"What's your name?" he asked.

"Maya."

"Nice name, that. But gotta go, ah? Wouldn't be right to make new ones for the rest of these bugs and not for you. Hmmm. What could you be? Tall, tall . . . I got it, you going be . . . try wait, it's coming . . . Zulu! Like those tall guys wit' the plate in their lip? Yeah yeah, Zulu. *Bwahahahahahah!*"

His laugh was loud as a weed whacker.

"Hey, Frankie," I said. "This is fun, but we gotta go home now."

Frankie was laughing so hard he could only
nod and wave us away.

Tito, scowling, said to Frankie, "We go, already."

Frankie stumbled off holding his sides.

"Idiot," Maya said.

"Got problems," Julio added.

Willy turned and spat, and Rubin slugged me
for laughing when Frankie named him Liddlebiddyguy.

"It was *funny,* Ruby."

He slugged me again.

"Ow! No hit so hard."

"Shuddup, then."

"Kay-okay, but he's funny, that's all."

Everybody stopped and looked at me.

"What?" I said.

Willy looked disgusted. "Are you asleep? Are
you even here? He just *robbed* us."

"You right about that."

"You right I'm right."

We continued on across the field.

I looked into my bag to see what was left. Two
Ball Park mints and the peanut M&M's. Could have
been worse.

Willy said, "We could take him, you know. All
us against him."

"Not if he got Mike and Tito with him," I said.

"I hate to agree, Shrimpy."

"Hey . . ."

As we got closer to the middle school we could see there was something going on up ahead in the parking lot. A small crowd, mostly girls, was closing in around somebody who was almost screaming.

We picked up the pace.

"Stay behind me," I told Darci.

"Joey, I—"

"Shhh."

"But I want to go home."

"Listen," I whispered.

Then I stopped and said, "No, don't," and covered her ears.

Because what we heard was somebody letting loose a string of the nastiest words I ever heard in my whole entire life, and even worse was it was coming from a girl.

We pushed through the crowd to see what was going on.

Ho!

The girl with the nasty mouth was facing off with a *boy*. She wasn't scared of him at all. In fact, she kept poking him in the chest with her finger, and each time he slapped her hand away, saying, "I ain't fighting no girl, I ain't fighting no girl."

Finally the guy turned his back on her and walked away, and all the girls cheered.

The poor guy was stuck. If he fought with her, he would be shamed. What could he do? Nothing. Just walk away.

And that's when the skyrocket went off in my brain, the idea that would save us from Frankie Diamond.

"Who's that girl?" I said.

Willy shrugged.

Julio said, "Don't look at *me*."

"Her name is Lynnette Piper," Maya said.

"You *know* her?"

"Not really. Her dad works with mine. I've seen her at the beach, at company picnics. She doesn't take anything from anybody, as you just saw."

This Lynnette girl strutted around smiling like she'd just won the world heavyweight boxing buckle. Of course, that made all those girls go wild. I wanted to ask somebody what the fight was about, but I thought it might be smarter to keep low until things settled down.

"Maya," I said. "Tell her you want to talk to her."

"Who?"

"Lynnette Piper. I have an idea."

Willy, Julio, and Liddlebiddyguy turned to look at me.

"No, really, Maya, listen," I said. "This Lynnette . . . since she's your friend, maybe you could get her to . . . you know, sort of help us out. Maybe she could become one of us for a day. I mean, look at her. She's small, like us. She fits. And when Frankie tries to rob us, she can tell him to go somewhere else, you know. Take a hike. Like she told that guy just now. What's Frankie going to do? Fight with her? See what I mean? It would shame him to fight a girl. He'd be stuck."

Maya stared at me a long time, then said, "First of all, Joey, she's not my friend, and second of all, you are so far out of your mind you might never make it back."

"Why?"

"Because she won't even listen to me. Why would she? She doesn't even know me. And anyway, I don't want her going after me for bothering her."

The crowd of girls started breaking up. Where was Lynnette?

"Come on, Maya. Hurry, before she leaves."

"I'm going home."

Lynnette made a clean escape. She simply wasn't there anymore. How'd she do that?

When Darci and I got home, Stella was on the phone. It was how she lived, you know? Had it jammed between her ear and shoulder so her hands were free to do other things, like maybe sand her fingernails or paint her toenails white.

"I'm going right back out," I said, handing Darci over.

Stella ignored me, like always.

I dumped my backpack in my room and headed over to Maya's house. I still thought I had a great idea. Lynnette was so scrappy Frankie wouldn't know what to do with her.

"Come on, Maya, call her up," I said when I got there. "She can help us. I know she can."

Maya looked down at me like I was some insect she was thinking about stepping on.

"Okay, then, just see if you can get her phone number. *I'll* call her."

"Do I look like a phone book?"

"Well, where's her house then? You know that?"

Maya finally relented and said she'd show us where Lynnette lived. But only if she didn't have to talk. Three of us went—me, her, and Willy. Julio and Liddlebiddyguy had chores.

Lynnette's place was twice the size of any of ours, and the yard was neat and clean—grass mowed, green and healthy, edged, not all ratty and brown with armyworms.

Maya waited out in the street, where she couldn't be seen from the house.

Willy and I went up to the front door.

"This is too weird," Willy whispered.

"No, it's brilliant. You watch."

I knocked.

Nobody came, so I knocked harder.

The door flew open. "What!"

Lynnette scowled at us, annoyed as a scorpion with its stinger curled up.

"Uh . . . we . . . we . . ."

I couldn't say the words. The look on her face suggested that this might not have been the best idea.

"Whatever you're selling, we don't want it."

She slammed the door.

I waited a few seconds, then knocked again.

This time when she opened the door, she took a step toward me.

I stumbled back.

"We're not s-selling anything," I said, putting up my hands. "We want to hire you."

"Who's we?"

I turned to Willy, but he was gone.

"Uh . . ."

She smirked, like maybe it amused her to see me so nervous. At least she had a sense of humor, which I could really have used just then.

"There's this guy," I said. "He—he always steals from us."

"So?"

"Well, we need a—a . . . we need somebody to sort of . . . you know, make him go away . . . like you did with the guy in the parking lot at school."

"You saw that?"

"We were walking by."

Lynnette studied me closely. "You want me to help you stop some guy from stealing from you? Is that what you're saying?"

I nodded. Exactly.

Lynnette's mind was working. I could see it in her eyes, looking at me but not looking at me, you know? Thinking.

"Do I know this guy?"

I shrugged. "His name is Frankie Diamond. He's in eighth grade, in your school."

"Eighth, huh?"

"Yeah, I think."

"Big guy?"

"Bigger than us," I said.

"Is he cute?"

"Pshh. Not to me, he ain't."

She laughed. "I was joking. Come inside. Oh, and tell your friend he can come in, too."

I turned and looked back.

Willy came slinking out of the bushes.

"Come, come," Lynnette said, waving us in.

We both hesitated. Maybe it was a trick.

"We need to talk, right?"

We went in. She closed the door behind us.

And locked it.

She saw us looking at the door and said, "My mom makes me do that. Someone broke in and took our TV."

We followed Lynnette through the house and out to the backyard. I couldn't believe it. She had a swimming pool, turquoise blue and clear as ice. A vacuum was snaking over the bottom with its pump purring like a cat. Man, I thought, I could move into this situation *today*.

We sat around a white iron table in white iron chairs with white iron arms on them. And you know what Lynnette did? She went inside the house and came back with three ice-cold Cokes.

Had to be a trick. This was too easy.

"All right," she said. "Tell me about this Frankie Diamond."

Lynnette met us after school three days in a row, carrying a math book and a spiral pad so she'd look like us. "I don't carry books," she said. "This is a disguise."

But Frankie never showed.

We did find out why Lynnette had been so nice to us, though—Maya. Lynnette had seen her that day we stumbled onto her parking lot fight, which we also discovered was just the end of a bad week with her boyfriend, now her *ex*-boyfriend.

The first day she met us, Lynnette said to Maya, "I remember you from those stupid beach picnics."

"You saw me there?"

"Of course. You were the only one who didn't look boring."

Maya snickered. "I know what you mean."

"One time I almost came over to see if you wanted to sneak away and do something intelligent," Lynnette said.

"Why didn't you?"

Lynnette shrugged. "Shy."

"Shy? You?"

"I don't make friends easily. My daddy says I'm way too opinionated. He said people don't like it."

Maya laughed. "That's what my mom says to my dad."

Lynnette tore a piece of paper out of her spiral

pad and gave it to Maya. "Here. Write me your number. Next time let's make plans to escape."

Maya scribbled it out.

Lynnette nodded and smiled and jammed it into her pocket. "We got to stick together. Only way to survive, ah?"

On the fourth day Frankie showed.

Along with the criminal brothers.

We had one bag of four-day-old saved stuff that we'd only nibbled at, since we were low on cash.

Lynnette looked just like one of us—short, and not nearly old enough to be an eighth grader. That's right, she was in the same grade and same school as Frankie Diamond.

But she didn't know that name.

Which is why when she first saw him she whistled low and said, "*That's* Frankie Diamond?"

"The one and only," Maya said.

"Ni-i-ice," Lynnette said, dragging it out.

"Nice like a stink bug," Liddlebiddyguy added.

"What's he doing with Mike and Tito? I know those two, and what I know ain't good."

"He's new around here," I said. "Maybe he just doesn't know who to stay away from."

Willy snorted in disgust. "Those brothers should stay away from *him*. He's the one robbing us, not them."

Frankie started toward us with his bad-news

grin that would be long gone after Lynnette got through with him. Mike and Tito, slouching along on either side of him, made it look like the gunfight at OK Corral. This was going to be something.

Yeah!

"So that's Frankie Diamond," Lynnette said. "I've seen him around but didn't know his name. He's cute."

I glanced at Willy. I didn't like the sound of that.

"Heyyy, Shrimpy-boy," Frankie said to me, walking up. He nodded to everyone else and added, "Whatchoo got for me and my frens today?"

"Nothing," Lynnette said. "Sorry."

Frankie's gaze wandered over to Lynnette, slow and amused, his white eyes smiling that magic that made Maya's heart jump. "Eh look," he said, turning to Mike and Tito. "The bugs went grow by one more since las' time."

Mike and Tito grinned. I guess they knew Lynnette and were thinking: This is going to be good.

Frankie walked up to face Lynnette, standing just inches away from her. "And what's your name, ah?"

"Does it matter?"

"No, cuz I going make you one new one, jus' like I did for all these liddle men las' week."

Lynnette crossed her arms, cool as ice.

"Let's see," Frankie said, posing like he had a

smart brain and was thinking. "As I remember, we got Shrimp, we got Mouse, Louse, we got Zulu and Liddlebiddyguy. Am I right?"

"Liddlebiddyguy?" Lynnette said. She smiled and looked back at us. "That's good. Who's that?"

Rubin scowled, glaring at all of us, who'd done nothing. But who wanted to glare at Frankie?

"You like that?" Frankie said.

"Not bad for one half-eye babooze, I guess. So whatchoo going call me, ah? Liddlebiddygirl?"

Frankie's grin grew when Lynnette broke into talking in pidgin English the way he did. He stepped back and looked her over as if he were just now seeing her for the first time . . . and was liking what he saw.

"Well," he said, his squinting eyes zeroing in for the kill, "I t'ink I going call you Liddlebiddybig-mout', how's that?"

Mike and Tito shifted and giggled, ribbing each other. Huh? I thought. They giggled?

Frankie turned to them and smiled.

"Big mouth?" Lynnette said.

Frankie turned back and studied her. "Yeah, big mout' . . . Cuz you liddle bit sassy, ah? I like that."

"You do, huh?"

"Yeh."

They stared at each other a long time, neither turning away, both of them grinning that bad-news grin, which Lynnette had down as good as Frankie. Maybe even better than him, and I had to wonder where a nice girl with ice-cold Cokes, white patio chairs, and a swimming pool got all that nasty talent.

Frankie snorted and turned away first. "So, like I said, liddle bugs, whatchoo got for me today? All this talk is making me hungry."

"I said sorry, remember?" Lynnette said. "Nobody got not'ing for you. Today or any day."

"Ah?"

"From now on."

"Ho, man, I *like* that sass," Frankie said. "But," he added, opening his hands, "don't mean not'ing to me, ah? You can talk, you can make like you big, but whatchoo going do about it, ah? You see? You stuck."

"Think so?"

"Yeh."

Frankie spotted Darci and winked.

Darci, who was holding the one bag of stuff we had, said, "Look, I got you a jawbreaker." Which she did. Bought it just to give to him because she knew he liked them.

She reached in and pulled out the jawbreaker and handed it to Frankie.

Lynnette said nothing.

Frankie took the jawbreaker and tossed it up and down in his hand. "Thank you, Darci, my liddle fren."

"We going now," Lynnette said, taking the bag from Darci. "Bye."

"Sure, you can go . . . jus' as soon as I check inside that bag."

"No," Lynnette said calmly. "We jus' going."

Frankie laughed and snatched the bag right out of Lynnette's hand.

Lynnette snatched it back, quick as a toad's tongue.

Yahh!

Frankie didn't seem to know what to do. Mike and Tito crossed their arms and waited, as if thinking: in your hands, brah.

Frankie tried to grab the bag back, but Lynnette was too quick for him. He missed and Mike and Tito giggled. I expected Frankie to explode.

But all he did was smile.

Lynnette kept on glaring at him, eye to eye.

Frankie stepped closer. "You like die, liddle-biddybigmout'? Cuz you don't give me that bag I going be force to step on you, ah? Not going be pretty."

"Oooh," Lynnette said. "I scared."

Frankie took that last step closer, so now he was just inches from Lynnette, face to face, but of course Frankie was taller so he had to look down.

But Lynnette, *sheee*. Not like Willy. She didn't stare at his neck. No. She walked right into those dangerous white eyes, and I prayed she would have the strength to walk back out.

Lynnette held the bag behind her back.

Frankie reached around trying to grab it, but Lynnette kept shifting it from one hand to the other so he couldn't get it without pinning her arms back. Which he didn't want to do, because, of course, it would be embarrassing. What kind of guy would ever bully a girl? See? My plan was right on.

Lynnette held the bag out for one of us to take. Willy grabbed it and stepped back.

Frankie grinned, as if saying, Forget the bag, then, now you and me got business. He tried a new tactic—belly bumping, walking into her, all the time staring into her eyes. It wasn't about the bag anymore. Now it was about something else.

Frankie kept walking into her, pushing her back with his chest.

And Lynnette, being Lynnette, bumped him back. No hands, just chests.

Ho! I wondered what Frankie thought of *that,* because I noticed for the first time that Lynnette *had* a chest to curve out under her shirt.

Boom!

Boom!

Lynnette held his gaze, an almost-smile hidden in the corners of her eyes.

I wondered if Frankie saw it, too, staring down his nose at her with his chin practically on his chest. But still he bumped into her.

Bumping, bumping.

Lynnette giving it back.

Lost in each other's eyes, never once blinking. It looked funny almost, except that I couldn't stop thinking that any minute now they were going to get mad and start slapping at each other.

Mike scowled. Tito stood with his arms crossed, turning away every now and then to spit.

The rest of us gaped, mouths catching flies.

Then something weird happened. Frankie and Lynnette stopped banging into each other and stood with their chests and eyes glued to each other . . . and I knew my plan had just died.

Frankie grinned his shark-white teeth. Lynnette let that hidden smile loose.

And the Andrade brothers walked away.

Frankie, with his chest still glued to Lynnette, turned toward us and flashed his best movie-star look. "Like I said, liddle bugs, whatchoo got for me today?"

Willy gave him the bag.

The whole thing.

Nobody peeped or complained or even hiccuped.

Lynnette put her hands on Frankie's chest and shoved him away. "I haven't had this much fun since I ate a sixth grader for lunch. That was back when I was in fourt' grade."

"Yeah?" Frankie said.

Lynnette snatched the bag out of Frankie's hand. "Wot we got, ah?"

Frankie looked at us and wagged his eyebrows. "I always liked bugs, you know?"

He put his arm around Lynnette's shoulder. She raised an eyebrow but didn't shrug it off.

"Hey, Darci," Frankie said. "Lissen, anybody ever boddah you, I don't care who it is, you come see Frankie Diamond and . . ."

He frowned and turned to Lynnette. "What's your name, anyways?"

"Lynnette."

He nodded and turned back to Darci. "You come see Frankie Diamond and his new fren, Lynnette, ah?"

Darci gave him a shy smile, so in love.

And that problem we had?

It had just doubled.

"Hey, liddle bugs," Frankie said, walking away with Lynnette. "Nex' time no forget jawbreakers for two, ah?"

"Yeah yeah," we had to agree. What else could we do? Together, those two would rule the world.

Unless maybe we could get the Andrade brothers to help us out. "Hey, I got an idea," I said.

"Forget it!" everyone shouted.

Fine.

Waiting for the War

About a mile inland from Pearl Harbor, Henry Long and Sammy Maldonado, two sixteen-year-old island boys, were trying to ride a horse.

Actually, they were trying to catch it.

To Henry the horse was a menace. It would just as soon kick you in the face as look at you, and Henry was kicking himself for having bought it. But he sure wasn't about to admit that to Sammy.

It was the old forgotten brown horse in the weedy pasture not far from his house. It had been in there for as many years as Henry could remember.

Now it was his.

But he couldn't ride it because he couldn't get on it, and he couldn't get on it because he couldn't even catch it. The horse had a mean streak as long as an aircraft carrier.

It nipped him on the shoulder. It stepped on his foot and kicked his shin. Henry couldn't even get a rope over its head, and he was sorry he'd paid any kind of money for it. But Henry had his pride and wasn't about to admit the horse was a mistake.

"The old man just ruined it," Sammy told Henry. "Because he never rode it."

"It ain't ruined. It's a good horse."

"What's so good about it? You can't even catch it."

"So. It just needs to get used to me."

"Or maybe it just don't like people. But it looks like a good horse, yeah? Check out its back. Straight, not swayback."

Henry glared at Sammy, who he knew had never been on a horse in his life. "You catch it then. You get on it."

"But I think you could ride it, if you're nice to it."

"*Nice* to it?"

"Yeah. Give it grass, pet it."

"You don't pet horses."

"How come?"

Henry shook his head. "You just don't. You brush it, you slap its side or neck, you give it apples and weeds and comb its mane, but you don't *pet* it. It ain't a dog. It ain't a . . . a . . . a cat."

Sammy shrugged.

Henry looped up the short piece of soft rope and stuck it in the back pocket of his khaki pants.

The horse had belonged to a nice but sly old guy named Wong. "Only eleven years old," he'd said. "Still young yet, like you, Henry. He just jumpy because of the bombs, yeah? Was too close to all those explosions. Even had one went off in this pasture. Over there. See the hole?"

Henry saw the indentation in the grass. That had been a bad day, he remembered. Lot of noise, lot of smoke, planes, police, sirens. Almost two years now since the Japanese planes came. Thank goodness it was only *one* bad day, and lucky the Japanese never landed troops like everyone thought they would. Really lucky.

"You sure you can ride it?" Henry asked Wong.

"Yeah yeah. Look at him. Strong. Spunky. Got a nice high step. I give you 'um for . . . hmmm . . . fie dollah."

That's what did it. *Five dollars.* For a *horse*! Henry couldn't pass it up.

"But I can only buy it if I can keep it in your pasture," Henry added. The pasture had plenty of grass, a cool rusty-water pond fed by a mountain stream, and a lean-to shed for when it rained.

Wong said, "Yeah yeah . . . for fifty cents a month."

Henry scowled at Wong, but he was thinking he could make that much easy, just by shining two pairs of shoes down on Hotel Street. "Why not," he finally said. He gave Wong the five dollars.

Wong had grinned.

And now Henry knew why.

"Try give it some grass," Sammy said.

Henry looked at him, thinking of saying something like, He don't want grass, you idiot, can't you see he lives in a *field* of grass? Instead he said, "What I need is a bucket of oats."

"You got a saddle, or you going ride it bareback?"

"I don't have a saddle."

"How come you bought it, Henry? You not a horse guy."

"Because it was only five dollars, and anyways I like horses."

"Just not this one, yeah?" Sammy said, grinning.

Henry spat, then rubbed his chin. "I'll think of something. Let's go down Hotel Street and shine some shoes. I gotta make some money."

"Yeah, good."

Henry looped up the rope and crammed it into his back pocket.

When the military guys weren't on their bases or maneuvering in the hills or shipping out to some Pacific island, they spent their free time on Hotel Street in downtown Honolulu. And what they did there was stand in line—for tattoos, food, movies, the laundry, bars, and girls. They stood in line for everything because there were so many of them. Thousands.

Sometimes Henry and Sammy went down there and made good money. It was easy, since all those army and navy guys were just standing in lines. Sammy joked around with them, made like he was real friendly, made small talk, trying to drum up some business. And Henry shined the shoes, snapping his dirty rag and spitting on the shiny black toes. They even talked with the civilian mainland war workers sometimes, who ran around with loud mouths and their flashy silk aloha shirts.

But when Henry and Sammy ran across a serviceman or a war worker who was by himself, they would close up like turtles. If it was a bunch of guys, it was easy. A bunch of guys was nobody. But when it was just one guy, then it was a person. And that was not easy, that was different, a person had a name and opinions they didn't want to hear.

The bottom line was Henry and Sammy didn't really like all those servicemen and war workers. Nobody Henry knew liked them. They hated it when somebody called them *boy*, or a *native*, or when they heard somebody complaining about being on *this godforsaken rock*.

Henry's mother, who worked at the pineapple cannery, said the servicemen weren't so bad, it was the war workers who were the troublemakers—the machinists, maintenance crews, assembly-line workers, and clerks. "They got a lot of money they don't know what to do with," she said.

And his father, who was a steelworker at Pearl Harbor, told him, "Downtown you got thirty-five, forty guys for every girl, so right off the bat they not very happy. So what do they do? They get drunk and fight, that's what, and you just stay clear of them, Henry. Stay away from Hotel Street. I better not catch you going near that place."

Henry and Sammy left the horse and headed down toward the bus stop to catch the bus to Hotel Street.

On any one day there were about thirty thousand men crawling around Hotel Street. There was no way in the world Henry's father could ever find him there. Unless he was down there himself. And if he was, how could he explain that to Henry?

As they walked, the road so hot you could smell the tar, an army jeep with three guys in it passed. Nobody waved to anybody.

Sammy said, "What you going call your horse?"

"Killer."

"No, if you call it that, it will think it *is* a killer, and once it thinks that, you'll never get on it. How about Brownie? Or Bucky, since when you ever get on it, it will prob'ly buck you off." He laughed.

"I like Killer better."

"I had a cousin named Johnny, but everyone called him Pee-Wee. Because he was so small, yeah?"

"And now I'm supposed to say, what's that got to do with calling my horse Killer, right?"

"Everything, because since we was all calling him Pee-Wee, he started thinking maybe he was too small for play baseball, too small for football, too small for work cannery, too small for—"

"Kay-okay, get to the point."

"He ended up as a bookkeeper."

"What's wrong with that?"

"Shhh. Can you imagine writing numbers in a book all day long? Drive me nuts, man."

"How come you said you *had* a cousin. He's dead, or what?"

"No, he moved. Mainland. Couldn't take it."

"Couldn't take what?"

"The numbers."

"Sheese."

"Here comes the bus."

It was full, of course. Every bus at every stop on every day was always sweaty full. But they squeezed onto it anyway, rode standing up, packed in like Vienna sausages. Mostly local people were on it, but there were also some war workers and a few military guys, who all looked young, some almost as young as Henry and Sammy.

One guy on the bus was crammed up close to Henry. He was snappy clean in his khaki uniform. Army guy, probably from Schofield Barracks. Henry liked his hat, tilted to the side like it was. The guy caught Henry looking and dipped his chin, Hello.

Henry turned away.

Later Henry glanced at him again. He guessed the guy was probably about nineteen. He had dark hair, almost black. And blue eyes. Henry hadn't seen that very often, black hair and blue eyes.

"Howdy," the army guy said to Henry. The guy was just trying to be friendly.

Henry didn't know what to do.

"My name's Mike," the guy said.

Sammy, who was standing right behind Henry, let out a small scoffing sound that said, Can you believe this joker is talking to us?

Henry looked down at his feet.

They rode for thirty minutes more in silence. Once, the driver stopped the bus and got out and smoked a cigarette. They did that because they had so many customers, they didn't care anymore how they treated them, and everyone waited on the bus, afraid to get off and lose their place. When he was done, the driver got back on and continued on toward Honolulu.

Half the people on the bus got off on Hotel Street, Henry and Sammy among them.

And Mike, who went off by himself. Funny he was by himself, Henry thought. Mostly those guys went around in packs.

"He likes you," Sammy whispered.

"Shuddup. You're sick, you know? You need help."

"Yeah yeah."

They walked around. It was hot, the street sending up as much heat as the sun. Everyplace you looked was jammed with uniforms, white for navy, khaki for army, everywhere.

"Let's go check out the tattoo shops," Sammy said.

"Which ones? There must be fifty of them."

"All of them got Filipino artists," Sammy said.

"You know, sometimes they do five hundred tattoos a day. You know what's the most popular? *Remember Pearl Harbor.*"

"How you know that?"

"I know."

"Shhh. You so full of it, Sammy."

"No. It's true. My uncle told me that."

He was probably right, since Sammy had Filipino blood.

"Hey," Henry said, "how about Savage?"

"What?"

"The horse. Call him Savage."

"Junk," Sammy said. "How 'bout Spats?"

"Spats?"

"He got a white foot."

"But he only has one."

"So."

"So you gotta call him Spat then. Not Spats."

Sammy frowned. "Sound like somebody spit something."

"The no-name horse."

Sammy said, "What did Wong call it?"

"The horse."

Sammy shook his head. "I still like Bucky."

A fight broke out in front of a bar. Men yelling and shoving. Henry and Sammy ran over to see. A war worker and a navy guy going at it, but two navy SPs broke it up before it got going. The war worker guy went off looking back and swearing at the navy guy, telling him he better watch his back.

"Look," Henry said.

Sammy turned around.

Mike.

Mike smiled when he saw them, then came over, saying, "Not much of a fight, huh?"

Henry still didn't know what to do around Mike, or any service guy who was by himself. He sure didn't want to talk to him. But he did wonder where he was from. Ohio, probably. Or maybe Iowa. They were all from places like that, at least that's what his father told him. "From Ohio to the grave," he'd said. "So sad. They're just kids. Farmers and grocery store stock boys. Come way out here to fight and die."

But Henry never thought about that. He didn't care where they were from. He just knew he didn't like them. Like the rest of his friends.

"Uh . . . yeah," Henry said. "The SPs broke it up."

"So," Mike said, then said no more.

Sammy turned to walk away.

Henry wanted to go, too, but the guy was just trying to be friendly and, well, he wasn't so bad. Henry grabbed Sammy's arm. "Wait."

Sammy stopped and turned back quickly, like maybe Henry was going to fight the guy.

Henry searched for something to say. Nothing came.

"I hate this street," Mike said. "Nothing's real, you know? Don't it seem that way to you?"

Sammy tugged at Henry's arm, like, Come on, let's get out of here, already. We got shoes to shine.

"Yeah," Henry said to the army guy. "But it's kind of fun to watch all you guys stand around waiting."

Mike shook his head. "That's what we do, ain't it? Wait. Wait for everything. Wait for a cup of coffee. Wait for a shoe shine. Wait for the war."

Henry hadn't ever thought of that before, wait for the war. Strange.

Sammy turned his back to them.

"What's your name?" the army guy, Mike, asked.

"Henry. And this is Sammy," he added, pointing a thumb back over his shoulder.

Finally Sammy turned around. He nodded, but cold, like maybe he'd rather spit than talk.

"He's not as bad as he looks," Henry said, grinning.

Mike put out his hand to shake.

Henry hesitated, but shook. The guy's grip was strong. That was good.

Sammy shook, too, reluctantly, and Henry prayed to heaven that his father wasn't watching from some secret hole in the wall.

"Where you from?" Henry asked, and Sammy threw his head back, like, Jeez, you gotta be kidding, come on, let's *go.*

"Tyler, Texas. Ever heard of it?"

"No. But I heard of Texas."

Mike nodded, then dipped his head toward the rope hanging out of Henry's pocket. "What's the rope for?"

Henry turned to look. He'd forgotten all about it. "Uh . . . oh that . . . I got a horse. Me and Sammy was riding it today."

Sammy stuffed a laugh.

"No kidding," Mike said. "What kind of horse is it?"

"A brown one."

"A brown one?"

"Yeah, brown."

Mike scratched the back of his head and thought a moment. "You think . . ." He paused, thought some more. "You—you think I could ride your horse? I ain't seen mine in six months."

That woke Sammy up. He grinned. "Sure you can ride it," he said.

Henry said, "It's kind of . . . well, it don't let no-body ride it but me." The last thing he wanted was to have this haole messing up his horse. And if his father ever heard of it, he'd—

"Got him trained, huh?" Mike said.

Sammy laughed.

"What?" Mike asked. "You boys pulling my leg?"

"No no," Henry said. "I really got a horse. It's just . . . hard to ride, that's all."

"Yeah, hard to ride," Sammy added. "We can't even catch it."

Henry thought, We?

"Bet he'd let me on him," Mike said.

"How much?" Sammy asked.

"What do you mean?" Mike said.

"You said you bet. How much?"

Mike grinned. "Okay. How much you got?"

That stopped Sammy, broke as a lizard. He waved Mike off, like, Forget it already.

"Tell you what," Mike said. "If I can't ride the horse, I'll give each of you five bucks. But if I *can* ride him, then you let me visit him once in a while. How's that?"

"You got a deal," Sammy said, sticking out his hand to shake.

"Hey," Henry said. "It's not your horse to bet."

"Sure it is," Sammy said. "I'm the trainer."

Okay, Henry thought. Fine. What did he have to lose, anyway? If he got five bucks from Mike, the horse would be free. He shook hands with Mike. "Let's go then."

Mike grinned. "Now you're talkin'."

The horse was way over on the far side of the field, standing in the blue shade of a mango tree. The air was still, no breeze, no cars or people around. Henry, Sammy, and Mike leaned against the rotting wood fence, batting flies away from their faces, studying the horse.

"He ain't a purebred or anything," Mike said. "But he don't look bad. Nice lines, nice head. He got a name?"

"Bucky."

"Not Bucky," Henry said, shoving Sammy. "It don't have a name yet. I'm still thinking about it."

"How long you had the horse?" Mike asked.

"A week."

Mike nodded. "Let's go take a look."

Mike stepped up and over the fence. Henry and Sammy followed him into the pasture, single file.

On the other side the horse stood staring at them, head up, ears cocked forward. When they got about halfway across, the horse bolted and trotted down to the lower corner.

Mike stopped and looked around. About two acres of grass and weeds. A few trees. He turned to the pond near the lower end, where the horse was now. "How deep is the water?"

Henry shrugged. "I don't know. Five or six feet. In the middle. I don't think it's any deeper than that."

Sammy said, "You got two five-buckses on you?"

Mike pulled out a small folded wad of bills, and Sammy's eyes grew into plates. "Don't you worry, I got it. But the thing is, I'm keeping it because me and that horse down there are going to get along just fine."

Sammy grinned. "That's what you think."

Mike said, "Stay close behind me, and walk slow."

The horse raised its head and trotted off a

ways. Mike stopped and the horse stopped, looking back at them. With his eyes still on the horse,
Mike reached back, saying, "Let me have that
rope."

Henry handed him the rope that was stuffed
into his back pocket.

Mike let one end of it drop, then looped it back
into his hand. "You boys go stand over by the
fence."

Henry and Sammy went down to the fence,
walking backward. "What you going do?" Sammy
asked.

"Make friends. Talk a little."

"Talk?" Sammy snickered, then mumbled to
Henry, "You heard that? He going talk to the
horse." He half-laughed, then glanced back at
Mike. "This I gotta see."

"Me too," Henry said. "The guy strange, yeah?"

Mike walked over to the pond. He studied it a
moment, then looked up. The horse was on the
other side of it now, watching him.

Sammy said, "Pretty soon he going see why we
call him Bucky."

Mike walked around the pond.

The horse headed away, not running, just
keeping a certain distance, with one ear cocked
back toward Mike. It snorted once and threw its
head.

Mike stopped again. This time he looked to the
side, not directly at the horse.

The horse stood waiting.

Mike walked away from it. Just kind of strolled off. And the horse took a few steps toward him. Amazing.

Mike stopped.

The horse stopped.

Mike walked, the horse followed.

This went on for a few minutes until the horse finally walked all the way up to Mike's back. But Mike didn't try to put the rope over its neck. In fact, he didn't even turn around. He just stood with his back to the horse. When the horse was only a couple of feet away, Mike finally turned and faced it. He said something softly.

"What he's saying?" Sammy asked.

"Who knows. Weird, man."

"You telling me."

Mike reached up to put his hand on the horse's nose. And the horse didn't throw its head like it always did when Henry got near it. Mike said something again, and reached into his pocket.

"What's he got?" Sammy asked.

Henry didn't answer, too interested in how Mike was taming the horse.

The horse ate whatever it was Mike had in his pocket, and Mike ran his hand along its neck. Then, slowly, he looped the rope around the horse's nose, making a kind of rope bridle. There was a name for it, but Henry couldn't remember what it was. Hack-something. Anyway, the horse let Mike do it, just let him.

"Look at that," Henry whispered.

"He still ain't riding it."

Mike led the horse over to the pond, then let the end of the rope fall to the ground. The horse stood still.

Mike took off his shoes and socks. He took off his hat and set it on the shoes. Then his watch.

"What he going do now?" Sammy said. "Go swimming?"

"Shhh. Quiet."

Mike unbuttoned his shirt, took it off. Then his pants and olive green undershirt. He looked back at Henry and Sammy and grinned.

"Look at that dingdong, standing there in his boxers."

"I think you're right. He's going swimming."

"Man, that guy is white."

"Look like a squid."

Mike led the horse into the pond, talking to it and easing it in slowly. The horse went willingly. No problem. Right in, up to its chest. Mike dipped his hand in the water and scooped up a handful, then let it fall over the horse's back.

"He's giving it a bath," Sammy said.

Henry frowned. What was the guy *doing*?

Then Mike leaned against the horse. Just leaned.

A minute or two later he threw himself up over its back, so that he lay over it on his stomach, like a blanket. The horse moved but settled down quickly.

"Ahhh," Henry whispered. "The guy is smart, very very smart. He going get on it in the water, where the horse can't run, or throw him off, or if it does throw him off, going be an easy fall. Smart."

When the horse was settled, Mike eased up on its back and sat, bareback. For a long moment he just sat.

Henry grinned. He liked what he was seeing. Someone could at least get on the horse, even if it was a mainland army guy. Mike was okay, you know?

Mike took up the rope bridle and nudged the horse with his heels. The horse jumped, then walked out of the pond. Mike rode around the pond. Rode up to the top of the pasture, then back.

Henry thought Mike looked pretty good on it.

Mike clucked his tongue and the horse broke into an easy run. Mike rode smooth on its back, and Henry could hardly believe that someone could ride a horse like that with no saddle and not bounce off.

"I don't believe it," Sammy said.

"The guy knows what he's doing."

"Unlike us."

"Yeah, unlike us."

A few minutes later Mike rode up. Stopped, sat looking down at them. "This is still a fine horse, Henry. He's a little old, and he hasn't been ridden in a while, but he's been ridden in the past."

"It wouldn't even let me near it."

"You just have to know how to talk to him, that's all."

"Stupid to talk to a horse," Sammy said.

"No it ain't. It's part of gaining his trust. After that, he'll let you ride him."

Sammy frowned.

Henry said, "Well, I guess you won the bet."

"You want to try riding him?"

"Nah."

"Come on. He's your horse."

"It won't let me on it."

"Sure he will." Mike slid off. "Come, stand here by him, let him smell you, let him look at you."

"Uhhh . . . I don't know," Henry said.

The horse twisted an ear toward him.

"Go ahead," Mike said. "Rub his nose, tell him he's a good horse."

Henry inched closer and rubbed the horse's nose. It was soft, soft as feathers. The eye was big and shiny. Brown. "Nice horse," he said, like you'd say to a dog.

"Good," Mike said. "Here, take the rope. Walk around, let him follow you."

Henry led the horse around the pond.

Mike and Sammy stood silently watching.

Out on the ocean two destroyers and a transport ship were heading away from Pearl Harbor. In the distance you could hear the faint cracking of rifle shot, men maneuvering in the hills. A plane droned by, silver in the clear blue sky.

When Henry got back, Mike said, "Okay, see if you can get on him. If he gets jumpy, you can take him into the water like I did. He likes the water. Come up and lean on his side, let him get used to you. Then try to get up on him."

Henry put his arms over the horse's back and leaned on it. The horse's ears turned back, then forward again.

"See," Mike said. "Now go on, get on him."

Henry took the rope bridle, grabbed a hank of mane, and jumped up on its back. The horse took a few side steps, then settled down. Henry grinned.

"See," Sammy said. "I told you you could ride it if you were nice to it."

Henry rode the horse to the top of the field, then back down again. "He's really *not* a bad horse," he said when he got back.

"No, he sure ain't," Mike said.

Henry rode around the pond two times, then came back and slid off. He took the rope bridle off and set the horse free. But the horse just stood there.

Mike went down to the pond to get his clothes. He was dry now, from the sun. He got dressed, and the three of them walked back over to the road.

Mike said, "So it's okay, then, if I come see the horse?"

"Yeah yeah," Henry said. "Anytime. Just come see 'um, ride 'um, whatever you want."

Mike grinned and shook hands with Henry and Sammy. "Thanks. I hope I can get up here a couple more times before I ship out."

"Yeah, couple times," Henry said. "Hey, what you had in your pocket, that you gave the horse?"

"Jelly beans."

"Hah," Henry said.

"When he does something right, reward him. Always reward good work, good behavior."

Sammy said, "Like when you guys get a medal, yeah?"

Mike looked down and said, "Yeah, like that. Well . . ."

"Yeah," Henry said.

Mike nodded and waited a moment, then nodded again and started down the road to the bus stop.

"He's not a bad guy," Sammy said. "For a haole army guy."

"He sure knows horses."

"Yeah."

Henry and Sammy were silent a moment. Henry kept thinking of what Mike had said about waiting for the war. Waiting for the war. He'd never thought of it like that before, all of those guys just waiting to go fight. They'd always just been guys causing trouble around town. But that was nothing next to the trouble they were waiting for.

"He might die soon, you know, Sammy."

Sammy shook his head. "A lot of them don't come back."

For the first time since the bombing of Pearl Harbor, for the first time since the three-day ship fires and massive clouds of dirty smoke and mass burials, for the first time since the arrest of his Japanese friends and neighbors, for the first time since then, Henry thought about how even now, right now, today, guys like Mike were out there somewhere dying in the war, going out on a transport ship and not coming back. Young guys, like him and Sammy. Just kids from Texas.

"I hope he makes it," Henry said.

"Yeah."

"But probably . . ."

In that moment, with those words, Henry paused, feeling something in his gut, like a dark thought unfolding—all those young guys were just like him, only they came from the mainland, from farms and towns and cities, coming way out here to wait for the war, to wait, to wait, to wait—then to go. And die. All of them would die, he thought.

Henry winced, then shook his head. He rubbed the back of his neck.

"You know what I going name my horse, Sammy?"

"What?"

"Mike."

"Mike?"

"After the guy."

"Yeah," Sammy said. He was quiet a moment, then he said, "Because why?"

"Because that guy . . . he going ship out . . . and he ain't coming back."

"You don't know that."

"One way or the other, Sammy, he ain't coming back."

"What you mean?"

"I mean he going get shot and die. Or he going live through things that going make him feel like he was dead. That's what I think, and it ain't right, you know? It ain't supposed to be that way."

"Yeah, but he could be a hero."

"Maybe. Yeah."

"He could."

They were both silent for a long while.

Finally Sammy looked back at the horse and said, "Mike."

"That's a good name . . . Mike."

The horse took a step forward, grazing. And above the green mountains, white clouds slept.

The Doi Store Monkey

"Rossman, listen . . . I . . . I'm sorry about the monkey, okay?"

. . .

"Rossman?"

Johnny Smythe slapped the back of his neck, once, twice. Then his arm. "I know you're hiding in there, so come out, okay? It's creepy out here, Rossman. And these mosquitoes are (*slap!*) eating me alive."

Stupid mosquitoes.

"Rossman, listen. It's past midnight, already. What do you want me to do? Beg? Okay, I'm begging you to come out of there and go back to the dorm with me."

But nothing came from the black jungle that edged the school. No rustle of leaves, no skittering insects, not even a ghostly whisper. Nothing. The only thing on earth Smythe could hear was the mosquitoes. And the nagging voice in his head. Worm, maggot, scorpion. Heartless scumbag. Yeah, that's you, Smythe.

Tsk.

"Could be black widows in there, Rossman. Or maybe the loloman. Yeah, what if the loloman's in that jungle with you?"

Hmmmff. That would make him think.

Smythe shuddered and looked around for moving shadows, remembering the crazy man. He didn't live far from here. They'd found him by accident—they being him, Riggins, Pang, and McCarty. Riggins thought the loloman was probably only about thirty years old, but he looked a hundred because his teeth were gone, at least from a distance it looked like they were.

This crazy whacko loloman, as they called him, lived in a broken-down one-room shed in the jungle. Riggins discovered him one afternoon during the second week of school when they were farting around out behind the dorm. They'd all crawled up on their hands and knees and peeked through the bushes. Smythe remembered how his hands had trembled with fear and excitement as he watched this wild-haired man standing in his doorway, scraping a fork on the door jamb to clean it. When the man went back inside, they'd all raced back to see if they could find Rossman and talk him into sneaking up and peeking into the crazy guy's house. Rossman would do stuff like that. He'd do it because he wanted friends. Any friends.

Stupid Rossman, Smythe thought.

But anyway, they'd found him and brought him back and sent him into the clearing by the loloman's shack with that big, fat, stupid, lopsided grin of his plastered all over his face. He'd just stumbled up and looked in the door.

Oh man, had that lolo guy gone nuts! From inside his shack he'd screamed at Rossman in some strange language none of them understood. Smythe remembered how Rossman had staggered back, looking more stunned than scared. Confused, disoriented. And that's all Smythe had seen, because he and the rest of the guys had taken off out of there, terrified that maybe the crazy man had a gun and would come out shooting.

Rossman was mad as a hornet when he got back to the dorm, and to avoid Riggins and the rest of them, he hid out in the jungle for three hours, hid right there where Smythe was now, slapping mosquitoes.

But Rossman got over it and soon came slinking back to the dorm, where he joined in and laughed about it with everyone else, just like every other time Riggins and the rest of them faked him out or got him to do something stupid like that.

But this monkey thing . . .

"Rossman! Come out of there," Smythe said, scowling in the dark. "This is getting old."

Worm.

Still no sound came from the shadows.

"Rossman?"

Smythe took a step closer to the jungle, but it was thick and dense and dark and way too spooky at night to go inside, and he sure as spit wasn't going in there to drag Rossman out. So he sat down just outside the bushes in the tall, cool grass, smooth and silvery in the moonlight. "You know what your problem is, Rossman? You try too hard, that's what. It makes you look stupid."

Was that it? Smythe thought. Was that really it? Or was that just an excuse? A smoke screen for a maggot? Smythe frowned and bunched up his lips.

He looked up at the moon, bright as a fresh pearl. But clouds kept passing over it, making the night blacker. Smythe picked at the long pasture grass, tearing blades out of the ground and ripping them apart. When his thoughts drifted back to the monkey, he ripped a whole hank of grass up and threw it and punched his hand. "Rossman! Come out of there!"

Jeese, Rossman drove him crazy.

Or was it guilt that did that?

"Come on, Rossman," Smythe said, now more gently, as if he were talking to a true friend, or to some scared kid. "Just come back to the dorm. I'm sorry, okay? We're all sorry."

So Riggins was a worm. I guess we all were, Smythe admitted. If you thought about it. Yes. Definitely scumbags. Okay, maybe Pang wasn't, because he tried to do the right thing by staying out of it. But the rest of us were worms for sure.

Prep school. What it does to you. Turns you into morons.

But it's weird, Smythe thought. Ever since he'd been there, he'd had more fun than ever before in his life. All the guys. All the cussing and insulting and joking around and being cool and stealing each other's love letters and cookie stashes and hanging out in the dorm with no parents to crab all over them. He couldn't believe that he even liked the Saturday morning white-glove locker inspections. And flag ceremony. And even Sunday chapel, for cripes sake. Not the kind of life he was used to, but he liked it. Algebra, geography, French.

Oh, and private lessons from people like Riggins on how to be a first-rate genuine-article blue-bellied zit-faced screaming-eagle scumbag.

"Hey, Rossman. Remember when Pang opened that reeking jar of kimchi in Mr. Chapman's class? Man, was that funny. Remember that?"

A slight rustle.

Or something. Maybe a black widow, rubbing its hands together.

Smythe mashed down the grass and made himself comfortable, looked up at the moon. Wait him out, he thought. For a while, anyway. There was a limit to this guilt. He hoped. Why don't you guys just leave him alone, Pang had said. He's just like that monkey, except at least the monkey can get out of his cage once in a while. Smythe remembered wondering what the spit Pang was talking about—at least the monkey could get out of his cage. What kind of mumbo jumbo was that?

The clouds moved away from the bright, glowing moon, leaving it alone in the sky. Smythe covered his eyes with the crook of his arm. Why couldn't he just forget about the stupid monkey?

And Rossman.

Who'd showed up at school a couple of days late. Classes had already started, and everyone was pretty much settled into dorm life. Being late like that would have made it hard for anyone. That's for sure, Smythe thought. I mean, you'd get the worst bunk and the worst locker, and you wouldn't know anyone, and you'd have a pile of homework to catch up on, and at that school they dished up homework like saltpetered mashed potatoes.

But for Rossman being late was only a small problem.

Very small.

You see, Rossman had some kind of disease or something. Smythe didn't know what it was, but they called him a spastic.

His body didn't work. His mouth was lopsided and he drooled. He slurred his words when he talked, and he was hard to understand. His arms and legs went every which way when he walked. But he didn't use a wheelchair or a cane. He just stumbled ahead on his own.

Smythe still found it hard to believe that someone had actually sent him there to live with a
bunch of idiot ninth graders whose parents had
kicked them out of the house because they were
too busy to raise them or they didn't like them or
they wanted them to get into some hoity-toity Ivy
League college and turn themselves into lawyers
and doctors and investment bankers. Jeese, so
funny. Could you even imagine someone like
Riggins as a banker? Embezzler maybe would be
more like it.

Anyway, Smythe thought, what were they
thinking when they dumped this Rossman kid into
the midst of us scorpions? Who did they think was
going to help him? Who was going to understand
him? Who was going to stop people from making
fun of him? Criminy, it was like dropping a fly into
a jar of toads.

At first Smythe felt embarrassed for him. He
looked like a goof, and everyone laughed at him.
Smythe laughed at him. Rossman even laughed at
himself. That's the kind of guy Rossman was, now
that Smythe thought about it. Someone who could
laugh at himself. Smythe figured it took a pretty
big person to laugh at himself.

Jeese, Rossman. You should have ignored us
from day one. Beat it, buttheads, you should have
said, and maybe we would have left you alone.

Anyway, the school was new, only about seven
years old. But the buildings they all lived in were
dusty old military barracks. It was started by some

bishop, but people called the students cadets, thinking it was a military school. Altogether there were about a hundred and twenty boys, all sent away to boarding school, to prep school. To another planet is what it was. At least that's what it felt like to Smythe.

The campus—Smythe half-laughed when he thought of that place as a campus—was a square yard, maybe four or five acres, way up in the mountains on the big island of Hawaii. A row of barracks edged the yard in a *U* shape. In the middle was a chapel surrounded by a grassy lawn. An American flag flapped high on a silver flagpole, with metal halyard clips that clanged in the breeze. Tall swaying trees crowded in and leaned over everything on three sides. And then there was the thick jungle behind the trees, where Rossman was now, hiding like a rat.

Anyway, the ninth- and tenth-grade dorm, which was in a bottom corner of the U, right by the flagpole, had two open rooms, each filled with bunks and long lockers that nobody locked except McCarty, who always had cookies from home that he hoarded for himself. Ninth graders were in one room, tenth in the other. The shower and bathroom were in between. The floor was wood planked and old and dusty. Steam radiators stood in back, like exposed plumbing, under windows that looked out into the jungle.

Right next to their dorm a square, green building called the Mess Hall squatted under the towering trees, looking like an old toad. Smythe thought that was pretty cool—Mess Hall, like in the army. It was there, on the day Rossman had arrived, that Smythe had gotten his first close look at him.

Smythe remembered being called to dinner by the bell. The bunch of them filed out of their dorm and into the Mess Hall. They'd all been assigned positions at long tables, each headed by a faculty member. Smythe and all the boys in school had been told they would take turns waiting on tables and cleaning up. And they'd sit when they were told they could sit, and they'd eat when they were told they could eat. They would say grace, say please pass this and please pass that, and most important, they would learn to tip their soup bowls away from themselves and eat like civilized human beings.

Smythe had been assigned to a table in back near the kitchen, and there Rossman stood crookedly across from him, waiting along with everyone else for permission to sit. Smythe figured Rossman must have been kind of nervous coming into school late like that, a thought that now made Smythe's guilt grow even greater as he lay under the moon remembering all this. He sure would have been nervous if it had been him.

Anyway, Rossman's hair was blond and cut in a close buzz, and his clothes were new. Smythe remembered the way Rossman had gaped across the table at him with his lopsided mouth slightly open. Not smiling, not glaring, just looking in this tilted

way, as if he were sinking on one side. Smythe
had watched him a minute, then looked down at
his hands, fingers laced together in front of him.
Rossman looked goofy. Smythe didn't know what
to do, how to act. He peeked around at the other
guys at the table and wondered if he was the only
one who felt that way.

The headmaster came in and told the boys they
could sit. Chairs scraped over the floor, and silverware rattled as all hundred and twenty of them
settled down. Dinner began, large stainless-steel
bowls of food passing silently from one hand to
the next.

Smythe noticed that Rossman drooled as he ate
and kept wiping his chin on the back of his wrist.
No one spoke to him or even asked him to pass
anything. But by the end of the first week of
school, he was the great oddity of the ninth grade
if not the entire school. Everyone talked about
him.

"The guy walks funny."

"Can you understand him when he talks?"

"Man, has he got B.O."

"God, how can you even sit next to him? He
drools. Sick."

"How come he's here, anyway? He shouldn't
be here."

Rossman often just stood in one spot and
stared at things, at people, at clouds, at spiders in
sticky white webs. He held himself up by his own
strange kind of balance, leaning at an unlikely an-

gle with his arms hanging down like an ape. And at night in the dorm he snored louder than a flushing toilet.

It would have been easy to ignore him, or at least avoid him. That would have been the easy thing to do. He was different. He wasn't at all like everyone else. We could've just left him alone, Smythe thought. And maybe we would have.

Except that Rossman wouldn't allow it.

Because, they soon discovered, Rossman had a personality. He was a person. There was a boy inside that crooked body. A boy who wanted to be just like everyone else. He wanted to make friends, he wanted to talk to you, and if you listened and tried to understand him, you could even have a conversation with him. It took some work, but it could be done. The thing with Rossman was that he tried harder than anyone in school to get to know the other guys.

A wispy cloud crossed over the moon, and Smythe humphed, thinking that Rossman tried too hard, actually. Anyway, how do you really get to know somebody you can barely understand?

Smythe worked hard at trying to convince himself they had tried. They'd let him listen to their jokes, hadn't they? And Rossman laughed at them just like they did. And they'd let him hang around, right? Wasn't that trying?

Right.

Smythe tore up another hank of grass and tossed it, remembering back to that Saturday afternoon after their first full week of school. He and Riggins and a bunch of guys were standing around talking and joking and spitting off the porch at certain targets, like spiders in webs or leaves, or long-distance targets out in the quad. After a while Rossman came out of the dorm and lurched over to see what they were up to. They stopped spitting, a little uncertain if they should go on, since . . . well, since Rossman drooled and spat all the time . . . because he couldn't help it. So anyway, they all decided in some unspoken way that they'd continue spitting. So what if it made Rossman feel bad.

After a while they got tired of those targets and started spitting at each other, laughing their heads off when somebody actually got hit. Pang got splattered first. Riggins lobbed a lugie that hit his neck and headed down his shirt collar. Pang wiped it away as if it were death itself, putting on a great show of disgust, which was easy to do if you got spit on you. Everyone, including Rossman, thought it was hilarious.

"You're gonna pay for that," Pang said, and went after Riggins, and since Riggins was laughing so hard, Pang caught him easily, and the two of them wrestled in the dirt. It was pretty funny, you had to admit. Even now, lying in the dark grass by a creepy jungle, Smythe smiled at the memory.

So anyway, soon Rossman wanted to get in on the action.

That was great news because Rossman was the king of spit.

Immediately everybody ran for it, not wanting to be washed by any of Rossman's abundant slobber. Rossman, being Rossman, thought that was great. Such power. Such friends. Such good guys. He stumbled after Riggins, then Pang, then Smythe and McCarty, lobbing lugie after lugie at whoever was closest. They all wailed with delight, dancing around him like puppies, moving in, moving out, giving him a clear target, then racing back before he could react, all of which were no great acts of courage because Rossman was slower than mud and his spit flew harmlessly to the ground. Still, he laughed and wiped his chin with the back of his arm after each shot.

Poor slob, Smythe thought. Wasn't even a contest.

Then Riggins spat back—and hit Rossman.

Rossman stopped a moment, as if to consider it. For a second all the guys fell silent. Then with even greater determination Rossman grinned and stumbled off after Riggins, who ran for his life.

Then McCarty spat, hitting Rossman on the shoulder of his shirt.

This time Rossman scowled. He was clearly at a loss in this game, clearly outclassed. He was a joke, not a contender. He tried to get McCarty but ended up getting more spit on himself, again and again.

Finally Rossman snapped. Sudden anger roared out of him in one long, slurred warning to get the hell away from him. Everyone gaped at him a moment, then walked off in a pack, calling him a spazmo and mumbling what a dork he was and why did he even come to this school and why wasn't he in some other kind of school, like a hospital for weirdos or something.

Smythe scowled in the dark as he remembered glancing back at Rossman and getting a full-on view of Rossman's middle finger.

That first Sunday Smythe discovered that they would all be going to church. Every Sunday. He'd never gone to church in his life and didn't have a clue about what went on there. He was told he'd have to wear a tie and a white shirt and a coat with brass buttons. So that's why his mother had packed those things. He found that he had one white shirt and a clip-on bow tie and a clip-on regular tie. So at least he was ready for it. Whatever it was.

Along with everyone else in the dorm, Smythe filed over to Saint James Chapel with his neck squeezed into a choking starched collar. But he was okay with that. It felt kind of cool to puff around in the brass-buttoned coat. Like he was important or something. Rossman scowled along behind them. He looked like a drunk, Smythe thought, the way he walked. And his ill-fitting coat and wrinkled tie made him look like he'd just been tossed out of a bar.

In the chapel Smythe settled into a long wooden pew with Pang, Riggins, and McCarty flanking him. They were pretty far back in the chapel, back behind the upperclassmen. In the pew just behind him, Smythe could hear Rossman blowing his nose. Riggins leaned forward to put more distance between himself and the gross nose honking going on behind him.

A tenth grader named Cunningham who was an ace keyboard player blew hymns out of a pint-size organ while everyone else sat there waiting for something to happen.

After a while a priestlike guy entered the room wearing a long black robe. Everyone rose when he walked in, and watched him float to the pulpit. When he got there, he stood looking out over his congregation. "Let us sing," he finally said, as if what he'd seen before him was so discouraging he needed a song to wash the sight from his brain. A black felt signboard hanging on the wall behind him told the page numbers and order of the songs for the service. Smythe flipped the pages and didn't find "Rock of Ages" until after everyone had already started singing. Rossman, singing in the pew behind him, slurred the words off-key.

When the song ended, the service started.

Smythe followed the crowd, kneeling on a padded bench when everyone else did, then standing, and listening, and reading out loud from a prayer book, and kneeling again, and sitting, and staring out the windows, dreaming of the beach and the hot sun and cool, wet ocean that waited for them that afternoon. Time passed. Clouds flew across the blue sky. The cows on the distant hillside paddock didn't seem to move at all, frozen reddish dots. Smythe sang, and prayed, and dreamed, and sat waiting for the unfathomable sermon to end, his knee bouncing up and down with pent-up energy.

"Boys, boys, boys," the reverend was saying. "If I can only impress upon you one simple truth, it would be this: The smallest act of kindness is worth more than a thousand good intentions. Think about that awhile."

At that moment Rossman sneezed, and Smythe felt a light spray of moisture hit the back of his neck. He flicked up the collar on his brass-buttoned coat and leaned forward, as Riggins had. Riggins started laughing, not out loud but silently giggling at Smythe's show of absolute disgust. His head was in his hands as he hunkered down below the back of the pew in front of him. And his shoulders shook, it was so funny to him. Smythe elbowed him, which only set Riggins off more.

"Let us read from the Bible," the reverend said. "Psalm nineteen, verse fourteen."

Smythe flicked his collar back down and fumbled for one of the blue hardcover Bibles in the book rack in front of him.

Honk. Honnnnk. Rossman blew again. "Sick," Riggins whispered, but Smythe ignored him, not wanting to get in trouble and miss going to the beach.

Pages ruffled and swished, and in a dull, murmuring rumble the mass of boys read: "Let the words of my mouth and the meditation of my heart be acceptable in Thy sight, O Lord, my strength and my redeemer. Amen."

After the service ended, the reverend walked down the aisle to the back of the chapel and waited to greet the boys as they filed out slowly, in order, from the front of the chapel to the back. Somebody cut one, and Smythe covered his nose with his coat. Riggins started laughing, so it was easy to see who'd caused the problem. But Riggins covered his own nose and whispered, "Jeese, Rossman, couldn't you wait until we got outside?"

Rossman ignored him.

The reverend was shaking every boy's hand as they passed on out the door, taking his time with each of them, smiling and wishing them well.

Which drove Riggins nuts.

After lunch Smythe left his coat and tie and white shirt crumpled on the floor of his locker and tore out to climb aboard the school's brand-new bus. He sat with Riggins, Pang, McCarty, and some other guys about halfway back. Rossman, white as a peeled banana in his swim shorts, sat up front behind the driver, who was Mr. Marshall, who Smythe thought was a pretty decent guy. From somewhere on the mainland, like all their instructors. East Coast mostly.

The bus pulled out onto the road and lumbered away, grinding down to sea level, an elevation drop of almost three thousand feet. Down near Kawaihae they turned left onto a crushed-coral road that raised so much dust they had to close the windows and sweat it out until they reached the beach. Just about every kid on the bus made a big show of gasping and choking and generally dying in the heat. But Rossman, Smythe noticed, just sat bouncing in his seat down the bumpy road.

Why did he keep thinking about Rossman anyway?

What happened at the beach wasn't important. But afterward was. Because that's when they discovered the monkey.

They'd all dragged themselves back into the bus and headed back down the dusty road to Kawaihae, a scorchingly hot, dry, and desolate deepwater port that Smythe had never seen before. The place looked so dusty and foreign that he felt as if he were in some movie like *Lawrence of Arabia*. He actually looked around for camels as the bus pulled over and sat in its own dust.

He followed everyone off the bus.

Smythe kind of liked the place. Thick, monster

heat. Light green harbor, still as a tidal pool. And quiet. Except for the sound of an occasional truck that rumbled past to the giant harbor storage sheds, the place was dead silent.

There was a store there. Just one.

It sat on a rise right off the road. Doi Store, the sign read. Smythe and the guys followed the rest of the boys up the steep driveway to go get Cokes and crackseed and Popsicles and whatever else they could find to satisfy their raging hunger before heading back up the mountain to school.

Smythe had just enough money for two ice-cold Cokes and a bag of peanuts. He bought them and went back outside. It was almost eerie how there wasn't a breath of breeze to ease the stifling heat. Not even the faintest whisper. Weird. The place was like science fiction.

He stood with Riggins and McCarty in a sliver of shade, munching and drinking and checking the place out. Smythe spotted Rossman making his way back down to the bus, moving pretty slowly so he wouldn't trip.

Rossman stayed in the sun too long, Smythe thought. His face was as red as an apple. Smythe shook his head as he watched Rossman inch down the hill kind of sideways, a strawberry soda in one hand and his towel in the other. Jeese. Dorkman didn't even have the brains to leave his stupid towel on the bus.

"Hey, look what I found," someone said, and

Smythe turned to see Pang standing over by something that looked like a cage. "There's a monkey in here."

The bunch of them slouched over to the large chicken-wire cage. Inside was a water bowl and a naked, well-worn tree branch. But no monkey, not that Smythe could see anyway. "Where is it?"

Pang spat out a peanut shell and pointed to the back of the cage.

The monkey was back in the far corner in a shadowy spot, still as an old shoe. "What kind of monkey is that?" Smythe said. "Just sits there."

It was one of those skinny ones, and it had a bare, red butt. The branch was worn so smooth Smythe figured the monkey must have been in that cage a long time.

"Rhesus, or something," Pang said.

Riggins said, "Somebody make it do some tricks."

Pang threw a peanut into the cage. It landed on the concrete floor, but the monkey didn't move.

The four of them hooked their fingers onto the wire mesh. "Stupid monkey looks half-dead," McCarty said.

In that second—*wham! bam!*—that half-dead monkey leaped at them, slamming into the mesh, screeching like it had just been shot with a BB gun. Scared the spit out of Smythe, who flew back. The monkey shook the wire mesh, shook it and rattled it, trying to get at them. Smythe's heart pumped like a piston.

The owner of the store came running out. "Whatchoo kids doing? Get away from there! Whatchoo doing?"

"Nothing," Riggins said. "The monkey's crazy."

"Get out of here. Go somewheres else."

So they left, mumbling on the bus on the way back up to school about the god-awful lulu weirdo psycho monkey. After they got tired of complaining and reliving the experience, Riggins called toward the front of the bus. "Hey, Rossman, we met your brother today."

Rossman didn't move, but half the guys in the bus laughed. The other half, the upper-class guys in back, ignored the remark.

"I could tell he was your brother because his butt looks like your face."

Rossman raised his hand, still facing the front of the bus, and flipped Riggins off, which made everyone roar.

One week later Smythe, Riggins, McCarty, and Pang were back at Doi Store, checking out the monkey.

Riggins was eating a fast-melting Fudgsicle. "Hey." *Slurp.* "Psycho primate." *Slurp.* He was about to say more when—*pthooth*—the monkey blew out a bullet spit-wad that hit the mesh in a way that splintered it into a shotgun blast of slimy, disgusting spray that splattered all over Riggins's hand and Fudgsicle, which was now poisoned.

Smythe, Pang, and McCarty nearly fell over laughing.

Riggins dropped the Fudgsicle. Almost instantly it melted into a gooey brown puddle. He hadn't been even halfway through it. "Ghahhh!" he said, so mad he hawked up a wad of his own and spat back. It missed, but the monkey went ballistic, banging and screeching and running around in circles, calling to the guy in the store to come get these creeps out of there.

They all took off.

On the way back to school, Riggins brooded about it. Just sat in his seat in a silent stupor. Pang slept, but Smythe and McCarty talked about how totally insane that monkey was, and how it needed to be castrated to calm it down. Riggins rubbed his skin and mumbled that he was going to die if that stupid bus didn't hurry and get him back to school so he could take a hot shower and boil the poisonous, cancerous spit off his arms and hands and T-shirt, which he said he might throw away.

All week long Riggins stewed about the monkey and waited for Sunday, when the bus would take him back down to the beach. He didn't know what, but he was going to do something to get that monkey. He couldn't think of anything, until one night he dreamed of giving it a jalapeño pepper.

"Someone gave me one of those once," Pang said. "Man, was it nasty."

"Good," Riggins said. "The nastier the better."

That week Smythe followed Riggins around to every store in town looking for jalapeños. But nobody had any. In fact, some people didn't even know what they were. So Riggins called his mother in Honolulu and asked her to mail him a couple. When she asked what in the world for, he said it was for a science experiment.

"Look what I got," Riggins said when the package arrived. He held up a jar of preserved jalapeño peppers. "One of these will make him sorry."

"I don't think monkeys eat peppers," Pang said.

"Maybe they do, maybe they don't."

"Ask his brother," McCarty said, snickering.

Riggins grinned and walked over to Rossman's bunk. Rossman was lying there reading his geography book. "Hey, Dorkman," Riggins said. "Your red-butt brother eat these?"

"Grow up," Rossman said, and rolled away from us.

"Stupid retard," Riggins said back.

Smythe laughed. But he didn't know why. It wasn't funny.

Pang was right.

When Riggins threw a jalapeño in the cage, the monkey picked it up, smelled it, and threw it back out. Dumb idea.

Pang, McCarty, and Smythe, munching peanuts and M&M's, waited to see what Riggins would do next.

"Smythe," Riggins finally said. "Gimme some of those peanuts?"

Smythe gave him a few.

Riggins broke a pepper open with his thumb and stuffed the peanuts inside. "It's the little seeds that make it hot, right?" he said. "Well, maybe he'll go for the peanuts and get those hot little things all over his fingers." He looked up and flicked his eyebrows.

"Hey, psycho," Riggins whispered. "You're the absolute ugliest, stupidest, stinkingest, sorriest monkey I've ever seen in my life."

McCarty snickered. The monkey stared at Riggins from the far corner.

"Hey," Riggins went on. "I'm talking to you. I got something better." He dangled the pepper from his fingers, then eased it into the cage, gently, so the peanuts wouldn't fall out. Then he threw a peanut next to it as bait.

The monkey blinked.

A moment later he scrambled over, picked up the peanut, and ate it on the spot. Then he picked up the pepper and ran back to his corner. He looked at it and smelled it. But this time he saw the peanuts and started picking them out.

Smythe glanced back toward the store, praying the owner wouldn't come out. Then he turned back and watched the monkey eat one of the peanuts. And another. And . . .

The monkey froze. Looked up. Dropped his jaw.

And went berserk—screaming, screaming, screaming, bouncing around the cage like a pinball, charging the mesh, slamming into it and shaking it, shrieking at Riggins, who along with Smythe, McCarty, and Pang, ran for their lives, laughing themselves to tears.

"I going call the police!" somebody yelled.

Back at school, when Rossman heard the jalapeño story, he went looking for Riggins, and when he found him, he told Riggins in front of Smythe and Pang and McCarty that he was the saddest case of a human being he'd ever seen.

"Screw you, Dorkman," Riggins said. "You can't even control your own goddamn drool, idiot spazmo."

Smythe winced.

Pang found something he needed to do elsewhere.

But McCarty laughed and walked off with Riggins.

"I got another idea," Riggins said to Smythe and Pang a few days later. He grinned and leaned closer, as if he didn't want anyone else to hear. "Spit," he said.

"What?"

"Spit. We get the monkey to spit at Dorkman."

"Why?" Smythe said.

"What do you mean, why? Rossman's a dork, that's why."

"He . . . he's not so bad."

"You're such a loser, Smythe," Riggins said. "You heard what that idiot called me."

"Well, yeah."

"You bet your ugly face you did, and if you think I'm letting it pass, you're as crazy as that stupid monkey. Come on, Smythe, don't be such a coward. God, it'll be funny. Listen, you got to get Rossman to come see the monkey, okay? He won't do jack for me."

"I don't know . . ."

Riggins gave Smythe a sour, disgusted look and said, "Fricken pansy."

"Okay okay," Smythe said.

"There you go," Riggins said, slapping Smythe on the back. "Hey, sorry about calling you a pansy. I was just mad, okay?"

"Sure."

That's when Pang told Riggins he should just leave Rossman alone, that Rossman was just like the monkey, only the monkey could at least get out of his cage.

"I had it wrong, Smythe," Riggins said. "Pang's the pansy."

Pang shook his head, and Riggins walked off with his arm draped over Smythe's shoulder.

Well, I sure got suckered into that, didn't I, Smythe thought, lying there in the dark, waiting for

Rossman to come to his senses and come out of the jungle.

And he had. Fallen into it like a slug of lead. Riggins got Smythe to sweet-talk Rossman back into the group, telling him they were all sorry about everything. And Rossman bought it. Smythe closed his eyes and shook his head, remembering that Sunday.

After the beach Rossman, Smythe, Riggins, McCarty, and a handful of other guys who'd heard what was going down all bought Cokes and candy and ice cream from Doi Store as usual, then gathered around the monkey's cage. Rossman, standing crooked, grinned and seemed to Smythe to be genuinely happy about being one of the guys again.

Riggins nodded to Smythe, and Smythe put his hand on Rossman's back. "Have you seen this monkey yet?"

Rossman, still grinning, said he hadn't and moved closer to the cage. Smythe pointed the monkey out, and Rossman smiled and studied the monkey. And the monkey studied him back.

Riggins mouthed to Smythe, Make him go closer.

Smythe frowned, feeling kind of weird, but said to Rossman, "Take a closer look. Here, throw him a couple peanuts." He gave Rossman a handful.

No one moved, just munched and slurped and ate like they were all at the movies. But Smythe knew they were all biting their lips to keep from laughing. Everyone knew what was coming.

Rossman said, "Here, mongey, mongey, mongey," and dropped a peanut through the mesh.

Boom! Bam! Wham!

The monkey flew at the mesh.

Rossman jerked back and almost fell over, and Smythe saw the look on his face and it burned into his brain, and even to this night, remembering it all in the dark, he couldn't get that face, that look, out of his head. Everyone whooped with laughter, having known the monkey would do that, whooped and laughed and staggered around bent over with exaggerated laughing pains.

The monkey spat a wad at Rossman and hit him in the chest. Rossman looked down at it. Smythe watched him wipe the spit away, smearing it with the palm of his hand.

"Ahhh, he touched it," McCarty said. "Sick!"

They all backed off, maybe hoping Rossman would chase them.

But Rossman just stood there, mouth half-open, looking back at the monkey, the terror fading, the sudden fright.

The monkey screeched one last screech, then ambled back over to its corner.

Still, Rossman didn't move.

And Smythe kept watching him. What now grew in Rossman's eyes? Rage? Sorrow? Smythe couldn't stop looking.

"God, Rossman," Riggins said. "You just going to stand there? Spit back."

The guy from the store came running out and everyone backed off, everyone but Rossman. The man waved his hands at him. "You go home! Go!"

Rossman looked at the man, then blinked, then slowly listed away.

He didn't say a word on the bus. Didn't turn around once. Didn't smile, laugh, or joke with anyone. Didn't even flip Riggins off when Riggins yelled something about if his hand was rotting off yet.

Again, Smythe laughed but didn't know why.

That was yesterday.

What a sucker I was, Smythe thought, lying in the grass. What a heartless sucker.

Now Rossman had disappeared. No one had seen him all day. Smythe remembered again the headmaster's scowl at dinner, his accusing, face-searching silence after announcing that Rossman was missing and did anyone in the room have any knowledge of where he had gone. And why. When nobody answered—not even with a cough—he'd walked out of the Mess Hall with the place so quiet you could hear the floorboards creaking under his feet.

It wasn't until after lights-out that Smythe re-membered Rossman's jungle place.

"Rossman," he whispered, now squinting into the black undergrowth.

Thick, mucky silence.

He has to be here, Smythe thought. In there with the toads and mosquitoes and worms. Where else would he go? Where else could he go?

Smythe looked up, watched the clouds cover the moon, heavier clouds now. Clouds that stayed there. A faint light spot marked where the moon was.

"Rossman . . . I'm . . . I'm really sorry. Please . . . come back to the dorm, okay? Don't hide out here. Don't."

Smythe realized that he was begging. Really. As if he were down on his knees pleading with Rossman to forgive him, to release him from his . . . his . . . guilt.

"Rossm—um . . . Brian . . . listen, things will be different, now. You have my word on that, okay? Really, I promise. Really."

No breath of wind fluttered the leaves. No crickets, no toads, no stirring animals. The blackened sky swelled and came down and enveloped Smythe in its eerie silence. Even the mosquitoes had vanished.

"Rossman?"

But Rossman never came out.

Because he wasn't there.

Never had been.

* * *

The next day they heard that Rossman had somehow made it all the way down to Hilo, fifty miles about, and, finding nowhere to go, had checked into the police station, where he was now, waiting for his parents to fly over from Honolulu to get him. And take him home, where it was safe.

Not one of them would ever see Rossman again.

Except Smythe.

Who'd see him every night, in the cage of his mind.

Angel-Baby

Okay, this is it.

I have this problem.

Her name is Tina Marie Angel-Baby Diminico, and no I'm not making that up. Luckily, she just goes by Tina. Both of us are going on to eleventh grade after this summer, but me and her go all the way back to fourth. I've know her longer than that, but in fourth grade we got into a big fight, so naturally we got to know each other pretty well.

A freak of nature is what me and my two best friends, Jimmy and Alton, used to call her. Because she was taller and stronger than all of us, and not only that, she had this way of looking down her nose like we were somebody's spit splattered on the street. So of course we didn't like her.

But that fight. Guess what it was we fought about? Tetherball.

This was when we were all still at the small

school down in Kailua town. All of us must have played that dumb game ten thousand times, always arguing about who won and who cheated and who was a liar and all that. It was good fun, though. Arguing was part of it.

But this one time was different.

I was there with Alton and Jimmy and three girls, and one of them was Tina. Me and her were up. We played a good game, and I won.

But she said no she won and I cheated because I didn't stop the ball before it wound all the way up on the pole. But I did, I blasted it around and beat her.

But she said, "Israel, you are such a liar."

Then my friend Alton said, "Forget it, Izzy. It's my turn now." But Tina shoved him back. Ho, he didn't like that. But she was bigger than him, yeah? What could he do?

Okay, till then it was only an argument. But then she said to me, "Listen, midget, you didn't see it. It was too high up for you, yeah? You so small your feet don't even touch when you sit on the toilet."

Ho! She didn't have to say something like that. So I said, "Yeah well you so fat you would sink a barge, you stupid freak of nature."

Alton gasped, I remember, saying "*ahhhhh*," and looking bug-eye because he was thinking she might kill me. But Jimmy was grinning like a shark.

Tina jabbed her fat finger in my face saying, "You going pay for what you just said, Shrimpy."

I slapped her finger away.

And that did it.

Boom! She slammed me with the pads of her elephant hands. Felt like I got hit by a bowling ball. I said, "You stinking Amazon," and I charged her, yelling, "You stupid, ugly girl Frankenstein!"

I remember I said that. Boy, was I mad. Us two hit hard and fell to the ground and rolled around like we were hugging, spitting and scratching and letting loose words that would make a gorilla go bald.

Then luckily for us our teacher, Mrs. Silva, showed up with a broom, slapping at us like we were dogs fighting over a rat.

The rest of that day Tina didn't talk to me and I didn't talk to her.

But in the days after I couldn't get any of it out of my head. It was all so dumb. I mean, fighting about tetherball? Come on.

Alton and Jimmy wouldn't let me forget it, either. I can still hear them even now laughing and going *"Bwahahahahah!* Izzy went fight one girl! *Aahahahahha!"*

Jeese.

So embarrassing.

Two or three days later I saw Tina at recess. She was alone for once, eating a banana on a swing. Amazon snack, I was thinking. Monkey meal. I glanced around. Nobody was looking, and Alton and Jimmy were playing handball on the blacktop.

So I wandered over and said, "Hey."

Tina looked at me with half eyes, like, You stupid or what? You think I like talk to you?

I said, "I really won that game, you know."

"No. You didn't." She was so matter-of-fact.

I said, "How come you so stubborn, huh?"

She grinned at me. "Me? I'm not stubborn. I'm nice." Which made me laugh.

She shrugged, tossed the banana peel into the weeds behind the swings, and sat there waiting for me to do something else. Shee.

"Okay okay," I said. "Forget the game. You won, fine. Who cares anyway? But still, it was stupid to fight. I mean, don't you think?"

And you know what she said? She said, "You're right, Izzy. It was stupid to fight. I forgive you."

"You *what*!" I said.

She held up her hands, saying, "Just kidding, little man, just kidding, cool your jets, already."

Ca-ripes, she always making fun of my size, but I tried to be big about it. So I sat on a swing next to her. Funny how after you fight somebody you want to talk to them.

Crazy.

But even crazier was this: We became really good friends that day.

In the fifth grade she sat at my table and showed me how to make those pointy-foldy things where you pick a flap and look under it and there's your fortune. But hers was fixed. Under every flap she wrote, An angel is watching you.

Huh?

And listen to this, one time in the sixth grade
Tina made me *haupia* for my birthday, Hawaiian
coconut pudding cake. And she made a card out
of pounded tree bark and wrote on it: *Just for you,
Izzy—from your best friend Angel-Baby.* I thought,
Angel-Baby? How come she wrote that and not
Tina?

Weird.

But the *haupia,* wow. My mom raised her eyebrows when I brought it home. When she tasted it,
she closed her eyes and said, "Perfect." She winked
and I frowned, and hid the *haupia* in the back of
the refrigerator so Alton and Jimmy wouldn't find it
when they came over to raid our kitchen, because
Mom was right. Tina's *haupia* was perfect.

But Angel-Baby?

And that's not all.

You see, for a long time now me and Tina have
been tight as twins. Starting in the seventh grade it
was like when she wanted to do something, she
called me. And if I had something going on, I
called her. We still do that, and that's all fine. I like
it. Alton says, "You just like her because of her old
man's boat, Izzy. Admit it. You like that boat."

Sure I like it.

Her father is a fisherman, you see. And Alton
and Jimmy know that's what I going be. A fisherman. Just like Tina's father, the famous Lefty
Diminico.

But the thing is—okay, I admit it, I get kind of

jealous about this, but so what?—see, Tina works for Lefty as his deckhand, the only girl deckhand that harbor has ever seen. And she's good, maybe even the best. She's earned it.

But still I get jealous, because she's so good, and it just comes natural to her. You know? Some people just have what it takes.

But anyway I have my own boat. So what if it's only a fiberglass skiff? It's still a boat.

You can find it tied up in the small bay behind the pier. What I use it for is when I get time off from my summer job, I take it out and anchor in the harbor. Then I practice my guitar, which I started playing in the summer before ninth grade. Besides being a fisherman, my dream is to play slack-key Hawaiian music at some hotel at night. So I practice. A lot.

But I have a real job, too.

Grocery-store bagger, which is not so bad. You get to see lots of people.

But mostly I sit in that skiff, where I can practice my brains out and no one can bother me or hear my mistakes.

Anyway, to get back to my problem.

One time last year us guys were sitting near the pool at King Kam Hotel. We only got three hotels in our small town. This was the one down by the pier. Anyway, I was playing my guitar, and Alton and Jimmy were nodding their heads to the music and checking out the haole tourist girls. Alton likes to think of himself as a loverboy.

It seems to work, sometimes.

So Alton says, "Hey Izzy, you getting pretty good on that guitar. One day maybe you really might play in some hotel lounge. I can see it. All the drunk guys going say, Play me one for my sweet, okay? Then they going stick five-dollar bills in your shirt pocket. You going get rich."

And Jimmy said, "Nah nah nah, Alton, that's not it, Izzy going play love songs to the freak of nature. Shoot, how come we never thought of that before now? Am I right, Izzy? Huh?"

"Shuddup, you dingdongs," I said, pretending I was mad. But I wasn't.

Alton the stupit laughed and slapped his leg, saying, "Mr. and Mrs. Freak, *bwahahahaha.*"

"Alton," I said, "if she ever heard you say that, you can kiss your face goodbye."

"You got that right, brah," Jimmy said.

I can admit it. Tina's *still* bigger than all of us, but so what? She's about six-one, hundred fifty, something like that. And all we ever going be is puny punks, prob'ly all our days. Standing next to me, Tina's a giraffe, but don't you laugh, okay, because right now I got that serious problem.

Because my story gets worse.

A couple weeks ago I was at the pier with Alton and Jimmy, as usual. This time I had my new Taylor 612 blond-face guitar with the cutout music box. I was trying to play "Ku'u Kika Kahiko" by Ozzie Kotani in Mauna Loa tuning with the alternating bass. Really sweet song.

Okay, anyway, while we were there, here comes Lefty's boat into the harbor, the *Angel-Baby II,* forty-five feet of bright white fiberglass glowing in the late afternoon sun. Tina was standing on the bow with the dock rope coiled in her hands, ready to jump off when they came up to the pier.

Listen.

She had on jeans shorts and a white T-shirt, barefoot. Skin like creamy coffee. Long black hair blowing in the breeze, and when she spotted me she smiled and gave me a small wave and kissed me with her eyes—ca-ripes, she doesn't even know what she's doing to me. Even then, before I knew what I know today, I thought man, how much longer can me and her be just friends?

Things were . . .

Changing.

I stood up and handed my guitar to Jimmy because I didn't trust Alton to hold it. I told Jimmy, "Don't let this bang on anything, okay?" And Jimmy took it and fake-tripped, pretending he was falling into the water. I nearly had a heart attack, the idiot bozo babooze.

They never let up, those punks.

I jogged over and Tina tossed me the rope. I wrapped it around a cleat, then ran back and caught the stern line and tied that up, too.

Tina winked.

The *Angel-Baby II* had two men and their wives on board. Lefty and Tina tossed the four fish they caught up onto the pier. Kind of a junk day, only four small kawakawas, or what the mainland guys call skipjack tuna, maybe ten pounds each. Lying on the pier they looked like stiff torpedoes.

Lefty nodded to me, then told Tina he'd be right back and took the two couples back to their hotel in his truck.

Tina said, "You want to help put the boat to bed?"

Of course I did. So I jumped aboard, yelling, "Hey, Jimmy, try bring me my guitar," and Jimmy got up and brought it over and handed it down to me. I took it and set it on the bunk inside the cabin, then came back out on deck.

Jimmy winked and wagged his eyebrows, and Tina saw it and said, "What, Jimmy? Got eye twitch?"

Jimmy grinned and untied the *Angel-Baby II,* then tossed the lines aboard. Tina started up the boat and walked it out into the harbor, and the water was so quiet and silky. When I looked back, Alton and Jimmy were getting smaller and smaller behind us, both of them just standing there, looking.

As Tina skippered the boat between the moorings I walked up the aisle and sat in the seat across from her. She turned and smiled at me, and kept smiling.

"What?" I said.

She waited a second, then said, "You want a job?"

A job?

"Sure," I said. "When you like me to take over?"

She laughed. Man, her teeth are so white. "Funny boy," she said. "I mean for a few days."

I told her I already had a job, and she said, "You call that a job? How about this? How about a little trip to Honolulu for dry-dock repairs? Daddy can't do it because of his hip."

I said, "What's wrong with his hip?" And she told me it was some old high school football injury coming back to bite him. He had to have an operation.

"I have to take the boat to Honolulu and fly home," she said. "Take about three days. But I can't do it alone. I thought ... you know ... maybe you could come with me. Want to?"

Whoa. Hey, I mean, think about it. What that meant.

I said, "Well, *yeah* ... sure ... but I don't know. When?"

"Couple weeks. Ask your mom. Or do you want me to?"

"I'll do it," I said, looking down.

My mom likes Tina. A lot. So she didn't even blink when I brought it up. "Sure," Mom said. "Go. You want me to talk to your boss?"

I couldn't believe it. Didn't she *see* how Tina was looking at me lately? Didn't she see it was dif-f'rent now?

But then Mom didn't know about the volcano.

That's right.

There's more.

Back in the beginning of summer the volcano blew again. It was all over the papers, but when Tina heard it on the radio, she called me. She said she and her dad were going to drive up and see it that evening, and did I want to come?

So they picked me up and we headed south in Lefty's smelly fish truck. I remember looking down from way up on the side of the mountain trying to see the ocean far below. But the whole world was as black as octopus ink. Except for up ahead, where there was an orange glow that looked like a small town was on fire.

As we drove closer, Tina's warm arm was pressing up against mine. And her leg and knee.

Ho, man! Every time I moved, just a little bit, she was right there, still next to me.

So anyway, an hour later we drove into Volcanoes National Park. The eruption was in an old crater. The fountain was shooting straight up and falling straight back down. It looked like a giant sparkler lighting up the night. I can still remember how every tree and rock was ghostly still in their sharp shadows. And you know how it's supposed to be cold up there, at that altitude? Not that night. It was like we were on Mars.

Lots of people had the same idea as us. Cars were parked bumper-to-bumper for about a half mile along the road. We walked awhile, then made our way through the jungle to the edge of the crater.

The air got hotter, and hotter, then *way* hotter.

When we broke out of the trees, it was like we were standing in a fire. The lava fountain was maybe a quarter of a mile away from us, and it was roaring and crackling like a sugar mill—or maybe it was the trees around us that were crackling. I had to shield my face with my hand, it was so hot, like you would if you were staring into the sun.

Lefty gave each of us a large ginger leaf with holes in it he'd punched out for eyes, and we put those over our faces. It helped, though the leaf almost melted and my eyeballs were sizzling. But who could stop watching?

I'd never in my whole life seen anything like it. It was so awesome to think that the earth was just a ball of fire held together by a thin, dried shell, and inside it was raging to get out, like now.

But the lava didn't flow anywhere. It just fell into the crater and made a giant cinder cone behind it.

While me and Tina were looking, Lefty walked off for a while.

Tina said, "This is kind of spooky. What if the whole crater blows?"

I said, "Yeah, but we'd never know it, would we?" And she said, "Probably not."

And that's when it happened.

Not the volcano.

Tina.

She moved around behind me and put her arms around me in a real soft kind of bear hug.

The top of my head only came up to her eyes. But she hugged me so nice and easy, and I was so surprised I couldn't even think of what to do or say, especially when she started rocking, just the smallest bit, side to side.

Ho.

I just let her do that.

Even though the heat from the volcano was frying me and making me sweat like a spit-roast pig.

I could see Lefty making his way back over to us, and as he was coming closer, Tina said, "Izzy."

That's all. Just my name.

We stood there, and all the time Lefty was getting closer and closer. When Tina saw him, she kissed my ear and let go.

We left soon after that because it was way too hot. But I was so far gone I didn't care where we were by then. I knew from that moment, and really for the very first time, that now we wouldn't be just friends. I didn't know what to do about that.

And that ain't all.

There's still the trip to Honolulu on the *Angel-Baby II*. It's weird, because it just keeps getting worse and worse. Or better and better, I don't know.

Jeese.

And that's where I am right now.

On the boat.

Just me and Tina.

Alone.

See my problem?

We left early this morning.

It was a windy, overcast day when we got down to the pier, and Lefty said, "Maybe you two should wait a day, let this weather pass."

But Tina said, "Nah, Daddy, we can do it."

Lefty looked at me like, *you* tell her, Izzy. But I just shrugged and said, "I don't get seasick."

He grinned and tapped my shoulder, like that was what he wanted to hear. "Fine," he said. "Go." Just like my mom. "But if you get down by Kawaihae and it's gotten worse, you set in there and wait out the weather, okay? I don't want you two out there in a nasty sea. I got enough to worry about with this damn hip."

Tina gave him a big hug. "Don't worry, Daddy. I know what I'm doing." Then she turned to me and said, "Let's go," and that was that.

We set out on that stormy morning with Tina standing at the wheel. She had a kind of imp look on her face when she checked out that bad weather, so sure of herself. I thought, Man, here we go.

When we got out past the lighthouse the world opened up, free of land, free of people. Just me and Tina and the sea. It was unreal . . . and so was the weather, in a bad way.

Now, ever since that night at the volcano, Tina's been on my mind. In my dreams at night she's kissing my ear and holding me in that soft bear hug, the both of us frying in the heat and not caring about it one little bit.

Wow.

So here I am on the boat, wondering if Tina ever thinks about the volcano like I do. Maybe she doesn't. Maybe she just felt good that night, or something. I keep trying to stop thinking about it. Impossible.

It takes us a couple of hours to get down by Kawaihae, where her dad wanted us to set in if the weather looked worse. Well, it does look worse, but not terrible worse.

Tina smiles and winks.

I say, "You gonna call him?"

"Nope."

A little while later she says, "Shall we see if we can make Lahaina by nightfall, or you want to check in at Kawaihae and make Daddy happy?"

What can I say to that?

So I go around tying everything down. It's going to get a lot rougher out in the channel between the islands of Hawaii and Maui. Alenuihaha, in case you didn't know, is one of the world's most treacherous ocean passages.

As we rumble out from the protection of the mountains on the north end of Hawaii, the wind smashes into us like an overloaded cane truck. It rises up and spits whitecaps across the ocean for as far as you can see, and the swells crank higher, and deeper, and it's as wild as I've ever seen it.

But it isn't really stupid to be out here. Not yet, anyway. Tina would not have come this far if it was. I know that girl.

Nothing to do now but wait and see what happens. Ride it out and pray some rogue wave doesn't roll the boat.

I think about Lefty. "Don't you think you should call your dad? He'll worry."

"No. He'll tell me to turn around."

I shrug.

"We can do it, Iz. I've seen worse."

"You're the skipper, Angel-Baby."

She grins real big. "Say that again, would you? I like the sound of it."

She *does* have a sense of humor.

By three o'clock the sky is as black as tire-dump smoke. We're fully out into the channel now. Behind us Hawaii is barely visible. Ahead is Maui, coming closer, growing more visible, but we're still way out in the middle of a very angry sea.

The swells rise up and we rise with them, then we slam down into the troughs between. Tina clings to the wheel with both hands, muscling the rudder to stay on course. I grip the seat across from her, gritting my teeth as the boat bangs ahead, pitching and rolling like a dead fly whirling down a flushed toilet.

Tina glances over at me. "Almost as good as the volcano, huh? Remember that?"

"Yeah."

I don't know about her, but the volcano itself isn't what I'm thinking about. "What were we doing there, anyway, Tina? I mean, you know . . . hugging and all."

I say it just like that.

She's quiet a moment. Then, "I wish this boat had windshield wipers like in a car, you know? This ocean is a mess." Like I didn't even say what I said.

Fine, I think. I don't want to know anyway.

Which is a big fat lie.

By five o'clock the channel is tossing us around worse than ever, rattling every loose thing in every drawer and nook and stowage cabinet on that boat. The racket is incredible, like if you take a drawer full of silverware and drop it on the kitchen floor every ten seconds for five hours straight. You wouldn't believe it. You'd just have to hear it for yourself.

Tina shouts over the noise, "It'll get calmer just as soon as we get into the lee of the island."

I'm ready for *that*.

Well, we make it, we slip into the lee where the island blocks the wind, and the ocean goes back to just being cranky.

We finally head in toward Lahaina harbor. It's about seven at night. It's already dark because night falls like a rock in the islands. The sky is still thick with clouds, but the wind has finally stopped and the ocean is coming flat again. I don't think I'll ever in my life forget seeing the lights on shore, how they reached out over the water, welcoming us in, and how I could hardly wait to get on solid ground.

Several yachts are anchored in the bay, and

maybe five more are in slips inside the breakwater. It's all so peaceful after what we'd just been through.

Lucky for us there are no boats docked at the pier, so we tie up there for the night.

Now, I gotta say, the quiet after Tina shuts down that boat is awesome. After a day of humming engines and rattling loose objects and howling wind and a banging, pounding hull, I'm in no-noise heaven. I jump off the boat and I don't want to get back on it, and I say that to Tina.

"Yeah, you're right, little big man, let's get off this tank and go get something to eat."

Lahaina is as welcoming as a fresh papaya. The air is warm, and the lights inside the stores and restaurants along the shore glow like yellow gold. Ho, man, talk about romantic. We just walk around, amazed at being here at all. And even when Tina takes my hand and holds it, I'm so happy I don't even think about what we're doing.

We find a small restaurant, a low, dark green, old-style board building with white-framed windows that edges the ocean. Candles glow in orange jars on every table. Soft Hawaiian music is playing in the background. We get a table by the sea, and after we sit down, Tina reaches across the table and grabs my hands and squeezes them.

"Can you believe where we are, Izzy?"

I shake my head. It's amazing, all right.

"I've never felt so alive in all my life," she says. We order and eat and talk about whatever comes into our minds. I probably won't remember any of it, really. Not the words, anyway. But I don't think I'll ever forget what I feel and see. Like, out in the distance there are two boat lights crawling along the horizon. And the music, Cyril Pahinui playing "Panini Pua Kea," so soft in the background. And a plane light slowly blinking across the black sky, now opening through the clouds, with a million stars in the infinite distance. And a small freckle just to the left of Tina's mouth that I'd never noticed before.

"Know what I want more than anything in the world?" Tina says, bringing me back.

I blink. "What?"

"A hot bath."

"Well, I could heat some water in the galley and fill up the fish box for you."

She laughs. "You are so funny, Izzy, you know that? And cute. I like you. I've always liked you."

I look down and mumble something.

"I have an idea," she says. "If I can't take a bath, at least I can jump in the ocean and hose off at the faucet on the pier. How 'bout you? You up for it?"

So we hike down the coast to where there's a beach and we can get away from the harbor water, which smells like boat fuel. At this dark beach we just walk straight into the ocean with our clothes on, our T-shirts and shorts. We go in to waist high and sit down in the water looking back toward shore. I think I'm in heaven. Maybe I am.

Back at the pier, we hose off in fresh water. Then Tina goes aboard and changes into dry clothes. Then me.

Afterward we sit side by side in the dark on the roof of the *Angel-Baby II,* looking out to sea with stars popping out of the black night like silver ice. A slight breeze rises up and cools my face. Funny how small things seem so big in these moments. I don't want any of it to end.

I have it bad. You don't *know* how bad.

And that right there is my problem.

Because then Tina says, "Izzy?"

Then she waits, saying no more.

She waits for me to look at her. But I'm kind of scared to.

Finally, I do.

"Izzy . . . will you kiss me?"

Yahhh!

I have no words in me to answer that.

"Really, Izzy. Will you?"

Finally I say, "I guess so, yeah."

"Good. Come with me."

She stands and reaches down to pull me up. I follow her down into the cabin. "Wait," she says, and goes down the companionway to the galley.

I stand alone in the aisle between the table and the bunk, thinking, Oh no, where am I going to sleep tonight? On the bunk? On deck? Or . . .

My hands start to sweat.

Then I hear music on the boat's sound system—piano, sax, soft drums, guitar.

Tina pops back up the companionway. "My favorite musician."

"Who is it?" I didn't even have a clue.

"Houston Person. Kind of a weird name, but boy can he play that saxophone. Listen."

It's the kind of stuff you hear coming out of restaurants and bars when you're wandering around the village late at night. I like it. For real. I *really* like it.

"Good, isn't it?"

I nod. "Yeah, sweet."

"What I want to do is this, Izzy," she says, then pauses. "I . . . I want our first kiss to be one we're never going to forget. I've been thinking about it. I came up with an idea."

She waits, letting that sink in.

Well, it's sinking in, all right.

I say, "And your idea is—"

"To kiss you from the first to the last note of my favorite song," she says, butting in. "The song is called 'But Beautiful.' "

You know what I say?

Nothing. Not one word.

Tina smiles and goes to put that song on. "Don't run away, now," she says, turning back at the companionway.

The song that was playing suddenly stops.

There's a pause.

Tina comes running back. Her eyes sparkle, like diamonds, like stars, like the sun on a stream.

A new song starts, a warm, tender-note piano all

by itself, and it's real dreamy. Sweet, sweet honey in my ears. Tina with those deep, smiling eyes takes my face in her hands and pulls me up close, and I swear there's a glow all around her, like sunrise.

Then when the sax comes in, she kisses me right when it starts. And, jeez, this makes me embarrassed, but her . . . her lips are so soft and smooshy they make my mind kind of go off, you know? Like peacock feathers, opening up and expanding into every color you could even imagine. I lose all my strength. And when I hear the deep bass and now the piano again in the background, my mind sails away like a lost balloon. I see lights and stars.

And . . .

And the sax plays on and on and on, so pure, so warm, so incredibly smooth, and all the time Tina's kissing me and hugging me and rocking ever so slightly with the music like she did at the volcano, and it's so good and so right and so real that something bursts inside me, like a door opening in a breeze, or a wave washing up on the sand. *Something.*

And I wonder if I'll ever be able to come back from this deep, deep place I find myself in.

Toward the end of the song a wave of perfect notes flings me way out over the ocean, only I don't fall, I just keep on sailing out and out and out, and if there really is a place called paradise, or heaven, or whatever—I am there. I'm in that place, sailing out so far I can never come back.

When the song ends she pushes away from me slowly and dries my lips with her thumb and smiles with those eyes, and all I can do is stand dazed in the aisle between the bunk and the table, and I can't speak or move or think or breathe, and anyway I don't even want to.

"Izzy?"

Tina waits for me to come back, to say something.

But I can't.

She says, "I know I'm not like . . . you know, like the most beautiful type of girl in the—"

I start to tell her how wrong she is, but she puts her finger on my lips. "Shhh. I know you and your friends call me an Amazon. It's okay. I don't mind it."

"I never called you that."

She cocks her head and says, "Really?"

"Okay, that one time. But that was way back and I was mad, and that doesn't count."

Her eyes flood, and tears spill out.

"Did I say something wrong?"

She shakes her head, then smiles and swipes a palm over her cheek. "No. I'm just . . . happy, you know?"

And I do know, I do. If I've ever known anything in my whole life, I know that.

We sleep side by side in our sleeping bags on the roof of the *Angel-Baby II* under the Milky Way and a billion blinking stars, because the storm is little more than a distant memory now, and the sky is as clear and deep as fresh water, and you can see into every corner of the inkiest, blackest, most mind-boggling, most impossible universe you could ever even imagine.

The next morning we get up at dawn and set out for Honolulu. As the *Angel-Baby II* hums past the breakwater onto the flat glassy sea, the sun peeks up over the saddle of land between the mountains. Color springs into the water, reflecting the cloudless sky.

I stand out on the stern deck looking back at the island, not thinking anymore, because thinking only messes me up. Forget thinking. The only thing inside me now is a feeling of freedom, as if I were some small perfect part of a much larger perfect whole.

I turn and peer in at Tina, sitting at the wheel.

She must feel me looking, because she glances over her shoulder and smiles at me, as if our being there is the most natural thing in the world.

I study her for a long moment, then smile back, then shake my head.

Angel-Baby.

She's as perfect as perfect can be.

See my problem?

Man oh man oh man.

Hat of Clouds

My brother Randy got two things when he graduated from high school: a full day as skipper and supreme commander of Dad's deep-sea charter fishing boat, *Iwalani*—and an invitation from his draft board to come on down and join up with the U.S. Army.

It was 1966.

Randy had been working on the boat with Dad since he was twelve, so he knew it every bit as well as Dad did. I knew the boat, too, but not in the same way. To me a boat was something that crawled around on the ocean while you watched the clock tick. To them it was a reason to live.

Like Dad, Randy was a fisherman. It was what he was going to do with his life. There'd never even been the slightest question about that. All he had to do now was do his time in the army.

But I had no idea what I was going to do with

my life. "Jake's still in his cocoon," Dad joked whenever somebody looked worried about me. "He'll find his wings one of these days."

I was two years younger than Randy and still had time to figure it out, according to Dad. Mama wanted me to go to college, which would keep me out of the draft, and, of course, I could study veterinary medicine, something she thought I'd be good at. I did like animals. But vets sometimes had to put animals to sleep, too, so I wasn't sure if it would work for me.

Anyway, a man named Chad Lewis chartered the boat the day Randy got his chance at the wheel. Dad gave Mr. Lewis a discount since he wouldn't be getting Dad's expertise, which is usually what you're paying for on a deep-sea charter fishing boat.

Another man came along, too, a guy named Steve. Dad picked them up at their hotel and brought them down to the harbor. Randy and I had the boat ready and waiting at the pier.

"Mr. Lewis," Dad said, "I can assure you that my son knows the ocean as well as I do, maybe better. He knows what he's doing out there."

"I don't doubt that at all, Cal," Mr. Lewis said.

He shook Dad's hand, then climbed down onto the deck. Steve followed, grinning like a horse.

I untied the lines and pushed the boat away from the truck-tire bumpers on the pier, then jumped aboard. Randy throttled up and walked the

Iwalani out of the harbor, the new morning sun glowing behind the mountain.

Dad stood with his arms crossed, watching us go. When I waved, he lifted his chin. I don't think there was anything he could have done to give Randy a better graduation gift.

A couple hours later we were trolling off the Captain Cook monument, heading south. Other boats had seen a decent amount of action back up along the northern coast, but Randy had his secret spots, places on the ocean he could pinpoint from markers he'd picked out on the island.

He sat at the wheel, looking as right there as Dad ever did. It was kind of amazing, really, the way he had just grown into his skin like that. One day he was a kid in school and the next a seasoned fisherman.

He'd asked me to go along as his deckhand. "You green as bad money, bro, but I need the help. Think you can do the job?"

"As good as you, any day."

He laughed. "You prob'ly right."

Mr. Lewis turned out to be a pretty decent guy. He was from Denver, and wanted us to call him Chad. He and Steve were about the same age, thirty-five or so, and were both on vacation with their wives, who'd gone on a tour of the coffee farms up on the mountain.

Chad and Steve spent the whole morning

sitting out in the sun, talking about places to put their money and watch it grow.

I wandered the forty-foot boat, trying to keep my mind from zoning out. I don't know how Randy and Dad could do this day in and day out for their entire lives. It was mind-numbing.

We were running five rigs, three fifty-pound flat lines, and two one-twenties pullied up on the outriggers to keep the lines from tangling.

We had one strike early on but lost the fish after fighting it for only twelve minutes. Chad took the reel for that one and was pretty cool about having the fish break free.

The big hit came later. At 2:48 to be exact.

I was lounging on the gunnel half-asleep when the rubber band on the starboard outrigger snapped. The rod leaped to life, the reel screaming as line raced into the sea. The rig jumped and jerked and bowed out over the water.

"Yeeaah!" Steve shouted.

The *Iwalani* sprang ahead, Randy gunning it to strike the hook deeper. Smoke poured out the exhaust. The wail of the engine was deafening.

Chad and Steve staggered aft.

Randy throttled down. The stern rose in the rush of backwater.

Chad grabbed the fighting chair to keep his balance. "This one's yours, Steve."

"You sure?"

Steve stumbled to the transom and yanked the rod out of the chrome holder, hauling back on it, striking the fish in an attempt to sink the hook even deeper—once, twice, three good solid pulls.

I unhooked the safety cable, and Steve struggled back with the rod and fell into the fighting chair. "Woo-haw!" he shouted.

"Jake, come take the wheel!" Randy called, running aft.

I hurried forward and slid into the skipper's seat, remembering how the last time I'd taken the wheel the boat hadn't responded as quickly as I'd expected it to. You had to anticipate, be ready.

I turned and looked back over my shoulder.

Out in the stern cockpit Steve was leaning forward, hanging on to the rod with both hands, line still whirring off the reel a mile a minute. He tried to pull back and stop the run, but the fish was too hot, too strong, too angry.

Randy and Chad madly reeled in the other lines, both of them hunched over, heads bobbing, pumping as fast as they could. I couldn't see Steve's face, only the tension in his back.

When all the lines were in, Randy got the kidney harness and slipped it around Steve's lower back, then attached it to the reel just as the fish showed—a blue marlin, a big one.

It leaped full out of the water, shaking its head, sword wagging in the sun. "Ho!" Steve shouted.

The marlin went under, line ripping off the reel. Steve pulled, trying to slow the run. But it was impossible.

Randy scooped a bucket of seawater out of the

ocean and set it next to the fighting chair. He got a large sponge and watered down the reel, which was hot from the tension.

The fish finally slowed and held.

Steve pulled back, gaining nothing. Not even a half inch. "Good God, did I get snagged on a submarine?"

"Prob'ly over six hundred pounds, my guess. Just keep the pressure on, make him work, tire him out." Randy sounded so much like an old pro it would have made Dad swell up with pride.

Just as Steve started making a few small gains, the marlin renewed its anger and burst away. Steve bent forward, shaking his head and fake-weeping at the great gulping yards wailing off the reel. From the angle of the line it looked like the fish was going deeper, down where the pressure was so great it made it twice as hard to pull a fish back.

Chad slapped Steve's back. "Hang on, pal. You can do 'er."

Randy stood nearby, frowning, probably worrying that the marlin would go straight to the bottom.

The back of Steve's shirt was stained from sweat pouring down from his neck and hair.

"Cool him off with some of that seawater," Randy said.

Chad soaked up a spongeful from the bucket and squeezed it over Steve's head, then water-cooled the reel.

Randy got the gaff ready.

And the fish club and knife.

I kept my eyes on the line, keeping it behind the boat. I wondered if we'd even see the marlin again, let alone bring it aboard, the way things were going. Sooner or later Randy would have to give Steve his best advice. But, like Dad, Randy would let the angler test his own skill first. It was his charter, after all. It's what he was paying for.

An hour passed.

For all the progress he was making, Steve may have been trying to pull up a fire hydrant. He swore every now and then, but that was about all the action happening on the back end of that boat.

Randy wandered into the cabin. Checked the horizon, looked at the clock. "You doing okay, little bro?" he said.

"Piece of cake."

He humphed. "If that fish goes any deeper, he's a goner."

"What do you mean?"

"Pressure. Be like sitting under a steamroller if he goes down deep enough."

"Well, what do we do?"

"I'm thinking about that."

We both looked back out at Chad and Steve.

The line moved toward the stern, the fish going down, down. Randy reached over me and throttled the boat forward. Did it real easy, so smooth it didn't even begin to bother me that he overstepped my part of the job. I was lucky. As brothers go, I got one of the best. We'd never in our lives been at each other's throats like some brothers I knew.

Thirty minutes went by. Forty.

At times Steve rested, taking one hand off the rod, then the other, flexing his fingers. And my neck was killing me from looking back over my shoulder.

Six o'clock came and went. The sun was low on the horizon, turning the *Iwalani* a brilliant gold in its light. I envied all the other skippers and deckhands already back at the harbor chugging cold beers and swapping lies. Randy went out on deck, then paced back in.

The angle of the line told us that the fish was straight down under the boat. "Damn," Randy whispered, then went back out on deck. I left the boat in neutral and followed him.

"Feels like a sunken barge," Steve said, now about done in.

Randy nodded, trying his best to keep the discouraging comments I knew were in his head to himself. "Feel any movement?"

"Just my guts working their way up my throat."

Randy waited a second, then said finally, "I hate to say this, guys, but we're prob'ly dealing with a dead fish here. Or if it's not, it soon will be."

No one said a word to that. It was a sobering thought, after all the work Steve had put into it.

"So what do we do?" Chad finally asked.

"We could try to vector him up. But that could take hours, especially if it's dead."

"I'll bring this thing up if it kills me," Steve said. "Let's do it."

"All right," Randy said. "You got it."

Randy and I went back into the cabin. He radioed Dad and told him we'd be out a while longer.

"Got something hooked up?" Dad said.

"Yessir, we do. Problem is, he's sounded. But we'll get him. Take us a while longer, is all. Over."

"We'll be waiting. Over and out."

Randy replaced the transmitter, smirking. "Kind of bent the truth a little, didn't I?"

"Did you?"

"Well, sure. This ain't going anywhere."

I slipped out of the pilot's seat, grateful to escape that job for a while.

Randy eased the boat ahead. The angle of the line opened and fell back. Moving slowly forward, he let the boat pull the fish up awhile, then brought the throttle down, reversed the engines, and started backing down on the line.

"Start reeling," he said.

I went aft and stood by the fighting chair. Chad looked at me and winked. I think he was having fun watching Steve sweat.

Steve reeled madly, taking in all the line he could. When he felt the dead weight return, he signaled for Randy to pull ahead again.

Forward and back, forward and back. It was crazy, I thought. All this for a fish.

We did this vectoring thing until it seemed to

stop working. Night had fallen and the ocean was black. Lights on shore winked out at us, a long line of them along the shore and a sprinkling up on the flank of the mountain above.

"It's alive!" Steve shouted.

"He's right," Chad said. "Look at the rod!"

Randy left the wheel and came aft.

The tip of the rod jerked, almost delicately, as if a fish were nibbling on the bait.

"Wee-hah," Steve said. "He's still alive."

Randy touched the taut line with his fingertips, feeling the movement, frowning. "No he's not. That jerking is sharks eating your fish."

Mercifully, at 8:35 Steve got the marlin up to the boat. It was a gruesome sight.

Stringy red tendrils of meat flopped off the back end, just beyond the gills. Looked like huge worms as Randy gaffed the whole mess out of the ocean and flopped it down onto the floorboards.

"Good Lord almighty," Steve whispered.

All of us stood gaping down on the giant fish head at our feet, its big round eye stunned in death, lifeless sword stabbing out. It was about the size of a fifty-pound bag of rice. Very little blood leaked from it, most of it sucked out by the sharks and sea.

After we'd seen enough, Randy tossed it overboard. It was too dark to see anything in the black water, but you could sure hear the sucking sounds of sharks ripping it back under.

Randy nodded for me to go in and throttle up. "Let's take her home, bro."

On the way back Randy radioed Dad and told him about the bad-luck marlin, then told Chad and Steve stories of how sharks are half-blind, and how if they surprise you by showing up while you're diving somewhere, you can sometimes scare them away by screaming at them under water. Or by punching them in the nose.

There were two things wrong with that advice as far as I was concerned: One is, how can you throw a punch at anything under water? And two, could I even imagine myself punching a shark? What a joke.

Funny thing is, Randy would do it.

It was peaceful coming in late like that. The harbor, the boats asleep at their moorings. The taste of the sea on your tongue, the smell of cooking steaks in the air. It was the part of boats I liked best.

I stood on the bow with the rope in my hands, ready to jump off as Randy eased up to the pier. Chad and Steve were back on the stern deck, drinking beer, feeling pretty good.

Dad, Mama, and Chad's and Steve's wives were sitting in the bed of Dad's truck. He'd backed up and parked it right where we'd be coming in, the bed facing the water. They looked like a bunch of my friends, having a good time sitting around talking story.

A couple of feet from the pier, Randy reversed the engine to slow the *Iwalani*.

Dad hopped out of the truck and walked over. I tossed him the line to tie off, then crabbed back along the gunnel to throw him the stern line. Dad tied that one off, too.

Randy shut the engine down and came aft.

Steve threw his arm around Randy's shoulder and looked up at Dad. "This boy here is one heck of a skipper, Cal."

Dad grinned and said, "Well, of course he is. I trained him myself. Except I was hoping he'd catch you more than a head."

"Hah!" Chad said. "You should've seen it. Gruesome."

"So where is it?"

"Well, we sort of did a catch-and-release," Steve said.

Dad chuckled. "One way to look at it."

"I think it was dead before the sharks got it," Randy said.

Dad shook his head. "It happens. Just sorry you lost your fish, men."

"Nothing to be sorry for," Steve said. "How many fishermen can say they fought over a giant blue marlin with a pack of oceanic sharks?"

Randy didn't look all that pleased, though. I knew he wanted that fish.

He nodded to me. "Let's put her to bed."

After Randy and I moored and cleaned the boat, Dad took us all out to dinner. The eight of us sat at a big round table at Huggo's restaurant, right by the sea, with small waves thumping up under the floor beneath our feet.

Even though we'd lost the marlin, for Randy it was still about as perfect as a day could get.

A few weeks later he came home from JohnnyBoy's Red-Top babashop with a bowling-ball head.

Army-style.

"Might as well do it now and get it right, ah?"

His new look had us all rolling, especially Mama, who said, "You look like a porpoise." Dad just smiled and leaned up against him, proud as a peacock. I rubbed my hand over the stubble on his head. "Feels like pig's hair."

He punched me in the arm, grinning. "At least I no get pig's breath like you, ah?"

He left for the army two days later, bald as a mango.

"What are you two boys going to do without each other to get into trouble with?" Mama said while we all stood around at the airport.

"I don't know about this pantie," Randy said, crooking his arm around my neck. "But me, I'm going to see some action."

"Pshh! You dreaming, bro. The only action you

going see is a drill sergeant giving you hundret push-ups for being ugly."

Randy shoved me away, then stuck out his hand to shake. I took it, and Randy squeezed as hard as he could, but he couldn't make me flinch. "Not bad," he said. "Maybe the army will take you after all."

The army.

I knew it was coming at me, the same as it came at Randy. You had no choice. Uncle Sam called and you went. Some guys ran away to Canada. I read about that in the paper. But how could they do that and leave everything and everyone they knew behind?

Still, the world was getting to be a scary place.

I'd never heard of Vietnam before the war started. Then strange new words started popping up every week, on TV, the radio, and in the papers—Viet Cong, Saigon, Haiphong, the Mekong Delta.

Though I could hardly imagine any of it, a wave of prickles fluttered down my spine whenever someone spoke of Southeast Asia. Like Randy, Vietnam was something I would have to face, too.

And soon.

Randy wrote to Dad and Mama several times from boot camp and a couple of times from the war zone, usually with a short note to me at the end of each letter. But the last letter anyone got from him was addressed to me alone.

He started out telling me about an operation in the village of Tan Yuen, then wandered off into whatever was passing through his mind, the whole letter in one long paragraph.

. . . A guy in my squad died yesterday. He took a spray of bullets in his lungs, less than ten yards away from where I hid in the brush. I held him, propped his head up on my knees—he was lying in the dirt, alone—there was nobody there for him but me. He stared up and said, "Please—" Then he died. This is a cruel country, Jake. Don't ever come here. There are scorpions, and cobras as deadly as the Cong. I'd like to napalm them all, hit everything that moves with Sky Raiders and Phantom jets. I'm not on earth, I'm in Hell. It's 120 degrees and everything stinks. This is a pitiful place. I can't even laugh anymore. Who cares, anyway?

The letter was wrinkled, as if he'd stuffed it into his pocket a time or two, and he'd written with a dull pencil, the words smudging into each other toward the end.

I walked down to the ocean with my dogs and sat out on the rocks for a long time after reading that letter. It made my throat swell up and hurt, and I didn't really know why. Maybe it was because I'd never heard Randy talk like that before, sounding so . . . empty.

I should have kept that letter, I guess. Just because it was something he wrote, a memory, a piece of his life. But I didn't. I couldn't. I burned it in the trash dump out behind our house and never showed it to anyone.

Not long after that a man drove up our rocky driveway in a white four-door Plymouth. It had been raining for two days straight, and mud was caked all over the tires and wheel wells of his car.

Dad was out on a charter.

Mama was in the house working on a new quilt, and I was sitting out on the porch watching the rain and playing my guitar, a dreary, lazy day.

My three dogs went off the second they heard the car drive up, running out and whisking around it, leaping up to see in the window.

I put the guitar down and called to them.

The man waited in the car until they settled down to an excited whine.

Mama came out onto the porch and stood next to me.

The man got out and hurried through the rain and shoe-sucking mud to the porch with his hat crooked under his elbow. Raindrops freckled his khaki uniform, spreading into dark splotches as he ducked through the waterfall overflowing our gutter.

"Wow," he said. "When it rains around here, it *rains*. Good morning, ma'am." Then he nodded to me, saying, "Son."

He hesitated a moment, glancing over his

shoulder at the clods of mud he'd tracked up onto the porch.

"Don't worry about that," Mama said. "Those dogs bring more mud up onto this porch than any of us ever could."

He nodded, half-smiled. "Is this the home of Mr. Calvin Liu?"

"He's my husband, yes."

The rain pummeled the mud and trees around the house with a constant *shhhhhh,* making it so you almost had to shout to be heard.

"Come inside," Mama said.

"No, no, I'm—I'm too muddy. My name is Decker, Corporal Decker, United States Army. I'm here about . . . your son."

Mama gasped and stiffened, and that scared me, I mean, really scared me. I'd been diving and seen sharks lurking in the same water as me; I'd faced wild boars up in the rain forest hunting with Dad; and I'd felt the earth quake violently beneath my feet. But none of it made my heart stop the way Mama did.

"Is Mr. Liu home?"

Mama shook her head.

Time seemed to vanish, every nerve in my body suddenly alert and on hold.

"I'm sorry to have to tell you this, ma'am. Your son has sustained a fairly serious injury."

Mama's hand flew to her chest, and he quickly added, "He's okay, he's doing fine. . . . It's just . . . well, let me explain."

I touched Mama's back. Heat bled into my fingers through the thin material. She fell into her chair, the one next to Dad's, where they'd shared a thousand red sunsets. She closed her eyes.

Corporal Decker said, "He was with his platoon near Da Nang, crossing a grassy field. The boy in front of him stepped on a trap and was killed. Shrapnel hit Private Liu's leg, just below the knee, and he lost the small finger on his left hand. But the leg . . . the leg was shattered . . . it had to come off, from the knee down."

Oh, no, I thought. No, no, no.

Corporal Decker spoke softly, with a warm, comforting accent. When Mama started to cry, he took his hat from under his elbow and held it in his hands. Rain drummed on the metal roof of the house and splattered down to muddy puddles in thin waterfalls. Corporal Decker glanced toward Dad's chicken coops, but caught himself and apologized. "Your place reminds me of home."

He put his hat back under his elbow. "Your son is doing fine, Mrs. Liu. He's at the 249th General Hospital in Tokyo. He'll be coming home as soon as he's well enough to travel."

Then, after a pause, he added, "If there's one thing I believe, it's that there's no adversity a soldier can't overcome if he's lucky enough to have people who care about him at home. Some don't."

Before he left, Mama took his hand and praised him for having the courage to do a job as difficult as his.

"Yes, ma'am, it's a hard thing, all right. But when I see that a boy has something to come home to, it makes it a whole lot easier."

Corporal Decker tipped his head and said again that he was sorry and that he'd be in touch. The army would help Randy rehabilitate, he said. "But first he needs to come to terms with his loss . . . that's the hardest part."

After he'd gone, Mama and I sat side by side on the porch for a long time without speaking. Then, through her tears, Mama brought up every foolish thing Randy had ever done in his life.

On a hot, blue-sky day more than five weeks later, Randy came home. Mama started crying when he appeared, leaning on a pair of crutches at the top of the stairs leading down from the plane.

Dad hurried out to help him down. Randy hooked his left arm over Dad's neck and held the crutches in his free hand. The left pant leg on his uniform was folded up and pinned short.

We were all there—me, Dad, Mama, and a busload of other people.

Randy nodded and smiled and glanced around quickly through watery eyes. His face was thinner, with cheeks that curved inward. His hair had grown back but was cut short and trimmed close around his ears.

When he saw me pushing in, his eyes brushed by, as if embarrassed. I put three strands of sweet-smelling maile around his neck and gave him a quick hug.

I tapped the side of his arm. "Some people will do anything to get out of the army."

Randy ducked his chin. "Yeah," he said softly.

When we'd given him all the leis we'd made for him, you could hardly see his face.

It wasn't until after sunset that evening that I finally got a chance to be alone with him. I caught him slipping away from the house and all the people who'd stopped by to see him.

He hobbled down to the chicken coops on his crutches, my dogs sweeping the grounds around him. The chickens were sleeping, the yard quiet and peaceful in the still evening air. Randy leaned up against the wooden fence.

I approached from the side and spoke softly so I wouldn't startle him. "Twenty-six of them now. Dad got that red rooster a couple of weeks ago."

Randy made a low scoffing sound. "Where I was, these things walk around the place like dogs."

We both stared at the shadowy chickens in the dark coop. The cool night air sharpened the iron-rich smells rising out of the earth. The dogs sniffed around a few minutes, then headed back up to the house.

"How about I cut school tomorrow," I said. "We can go fishing out past the airport—take a cooler, spend a few hours."

His shoulders jiggled, laughing silently.

"What's so funny?"

"You want to go fishing—what a joke!"

"Huh?"

"A *joke,* I said!" He spat the word.

He took one of his crutches and slammed it against the fence. All twenty-six chickens rose up squawking and fluttering. Randy hit the fence again, and then threw the crutch into the mud.

He raised the other crutch to throw that, too, but I caught his arm. "Randy, stop!"

"What do *you* know about it, ah? Nothing, you don't know nothing."

Just then Dad came jogging down from the house. "What's going on out here? I heard the chickens."

Randy yanked his arm out of my grip. Dad looked at the crutch lying in the mud.

Randy turned away, hopping on one foot, then with the remaining crutch, made his way back to the house. I picked up the crutch in the mud.

"Damn," Dad whispered. "If I could just do something . . . anything."

I wiped mud off the crutch, then scraped my fingers on the fence. "All I did was ask him if he wanted to go fishing."

Up ahead Randy skirted the front porch and went around back, probably to sneak into his room unseen. I didn't blame him. I wouldn't be in the mood for all those people, either.

Dad put his arm across my shoulders as we walked back up to the house. "It's not your fault,

Jake. And Randy knows that. He's just . . . I don't know. Damn war."

War.

The word alone caused the hair on my neck to prickle. It was growing larger every day, bearing down on me, dark on the horizon—the mysterious names of each new Vietnamese town now carrying images of shredded jungles, charred villages, and boys my age without legs.

And I'd soon be asked to go there.

Dad and I sat out on the porch. "Remember old man Nakamura?" he said.

I nodded, staring out into the dark night.

"Lost every finger on his right hand when some monster fish grabbed the small tuna he had on his hand line. Cut 'um right off—one, two, three, four."

I winced. I knew the story, but still it made me sick to think of it.

"But after his hand healed, he went right on fishing like always. He just had to learn new ways to get the line up, that's all."

Dad sat silently a moment, as if he'd said it all to himself. Then he added, "Randy will figure something out."

"I still can't believe he lost a leg. . . ."

After a moment Dad said, "I don't suppose he can either, son."

After school I usually found Randy sitting alone on the porch with his .22 caliber rifle. Once,

as I walked up our rocky drive, he shot and
wounded a dove. It flopped around in the dirt
down near the chicken coops. He shot at it five or
six times before it stopped flipping.

The dogs, who'd run out to greet me, scurried
back under the house.

"What did you do that for?" I said, walking up.

"Do what, brother?"

"Shoot the bird."

"Why not?"

I didn't like the way he said "brother," kind of
spitting it with glazed, lifeless eyes. I may as well
have been some annoying tourist. "You've never
shot birds in your life," I said.

"Well, now I can, ah? Got plenty time."

Randy stood the rifle butt on his hip, barrel to
the sky, finger on the trigger guard.

Then he held the rifle out to me. "Take a shot,
little bro. See if you can hit it. Already dead, ah? So
you won't hurt it."

I started into the house. "I don't shoot birds,
dead or alive. I got things to do."

Randy lowered the rifle and turned toward the
dead bird. He raised it again and aimed with one
hand. A puff of dust exploded a few feet away
from the lifeless dove.

Three weeks later the *Iwalani* sat alongside
the pier, riding the slow wide swells that moved
into the harbor and thumped up against the sea-

wall. The sky was clear and the water blue-green in the afternoon sun. Dad was on board, working on the engine.

I sat on the pier with my spinner, gazing across the harbor to the island: the small village lined with palm trees; the old royal palace guarding a small sandy cove; the steeple of the first mission-ary church; Kona Inn with its long iron-red roof poking through the coconut trees; a lazy town peeking over the seawall. I would never have told a soul, but I was thanking God that I hadn't seen what Randy had seen. I didn't want to believe there was any other world than the one that ex-isted right there in front of me.

I cringed, wondering how I was going to take it when, too soon, the army would come knocking on my door, too.

"Jake!"

Dad stood on the stern deck of the *Iwalani* with one hand on the cabin roof. "Come on the boat for a minute, will you?"

I stowed my spinner in the back of Dad's truck, then climbed down onto the boat and sat at the cabin table across from him.

"I've been thinking about Randy," Dad said. "Sitting around the house all day, doing nothing but letting his beard grow, shooting his rifle at any-thing that moves."

I nodded. "I know. Whenever I try to bring up things to do, he either doesn't listen or tells me it isn't like it used to be anymore."

Dad leaned on the table with his fingers laced together. "Jake, listen. I want you to try to get him to come down here. He won't listen to any of my advice, and maybe that's my fault, I don't know. But I'm thinking maybe if we can get him out on the boat, it might bring him around. Maybe not, too. But we can't just sit around and watch him sink."

The ocean lapped and plopped against the side of the boat. "I can try, Dad. I guess."

"We can fish, just you, me, and him. You think Randy will go for that?"

"If he doesn't, then he's too far gone for anything. Before the army he'd have sold me to a tourist for a quarter to get to do that."

"How about Sunday?"

"All right."

When I got home I found Mama sitting in the kitchen peeling mangoes and slicing them into a bowl.

"Where's Randy?" I said, flopping down across from her.

"In his room."

I started to push myself up, but Mama said, "Wait, he's sleeping."

"Sleeping? It's three in the afternoon."

"He sat out on the porch half the night," Mama said, handing me a slice of mango on the knife blade.

I took it and thought for a minute, savoring the sweet mango. "I guess I'll go for a walk with the dogs."

"Wait, take Randy with you. It's time he got up anyway. Go, wake him . . . he may not show it, Jake, but he's always glad to see you."

I pushed myself up. "I used to believe that."

Randy's room was dark and smelled like stale sweat. He'd cut up an old cardboard box and taped it over the one window in the room. He lay on his back wearing only a pair of army-green boxers, the crook of his right arm covering his eyes. The .22 rested beside him. The skin on his left knee, where the leg ended, was dark and gnarled like a twisted root.

I quickly looked away.

"What do you want, pig breath?" he said without moving his arm. His beard was thick around the jaw and moustache, but splotchy in the cheeks. He didn't look like Randy at all.

"You going to sleep all day?" I said.

"Do you care?"

Randy may have looked a mess, but his room was immaculate. His shell collection was symmetrically regimented along two long shelves, from his large spiral conch down to the miniature pearl-colored auger he'd found off White Sands Beach. The surface of his desk was bare, the chair centered under it.

"Listen," I said. "Dad doesn't have a charter this Sunday. . . . He said he'd take us out. Fishing's pretty good now."

Randy took his arm off his face, sat up, and rubbed his eyes. "What? Are you blind? How do you suppose I can catch any damn thing with one leg gone, ah? Answer me that."

"Since when do you need two legs to reel in a line?" I folded my arms and looked around the room, then added, "This place stinks."

Randy snorted. "I like it."

"Listen," I said. "All you need is balance. Put your foot in the middle of the footrest, that's all."

"Pshh," Randy spat. "You have no idea, man."

"What if I make something to fit between your knee and the footrest, so you can use both legs?"

Randy pushed himself up and hopped over to the wall where his crutches stood, then went back for his rifle. "Come," he said.

I followed him out to the porch. Mama said "good morning" from the kitchen, but he ignored her.

Outside he squinted against the white afternoon sky, then crutched himself down past the end of the chicken coops. "Birds don't come near the house anymore," he said.

On the far side, where he couldn't be seen from the house, Randy leaned his crutches up against one of the chicken coops and settled down onto a wooden box that he'd brought down and set up. He took the rifle and pointed into the mango tree at the edge of Silva's pasture. "See that mynah bird on the right? The lower branch?"

"What are you shooting all the birds for?"

Randy held still, then shot the bird. Five or six other birds flew out of the tree. He handed me the rifle. "You shoot one."

"I told you before, I don't shoot birds."

He put the butt of the rifle on the ground and his hand around the barrel.

In our silence the birds came back and settled into the tree.

"What about Sunday?" I asked.

Randy jerked the rifle off the ground and threw it to me. "Okay, I'll go. But first you going shoot a bird." He glared at me.

I turned and raised the rifle. It was well oiled, and the small bullet pumped easily into the chamber. The bird was just minding its own business when I hit it.

"You happy now? Ah? You happy to see that bird die? Make you feel better?"

Randy grinned and reached for the rifle.

Before I gave it back, I pumped bullets into it, one after another, and blasted them into the ground around the tree, chasing the birds away for the rest of the afternoon.

I threw him the rifle and left.

Mama came out on the porch. "What's going on out here? What's all that shooting?"

I strode by without looking up. "Ask whoever that is out there behind the chicken coops."

At eight o'clock on Sunday morning I was sitting in the stern cockpit of the *Iwalani* with gallons of clean ocean air pouring into my face.

Randy sat stiffly at the table in the cabin. He'd

hardly said a word all morning. His .22 stood nearby, wedged between the bunk and the cooler.

Behind us four big-game lures skipped and twirled in the wake. The massive island grew bluer as we trolled away from it.

Dad sat sideways behind the wheel, talking in secret code on the radio with his friend Luther, skipper of the *Darnell-C*.

Luther said, "Ho, you should see Mauna Kea, hazy blue, sleeping under a hat of clouds . . . nice like that," which meant there were a zillion birds on the southern fishing grounds due west of the long, green, rectangular pasture high on the rising face of the mountain. "Clouds" meant birds, "nice" meant active—fish were biting. Dad and Luther changed their codes every week to keep radio eavesdroppers confused. Dad slowly headed the boat south so as not to draw too much attention if anyone was watching him.

Someday Randy would have to get a real fake leg, I suppose. But for now it was either watch him hop around on one foot, or make him something. So all that week I'd worked in the garage on a contraption that Randy could stick on the end of his leg so that he could have the support of both legs in fighting a big fish. I set a two-by-two into Dad's lathe and carved out a stick-leg with a twirly design on it, kind of like a fancy table leg, only my leg was kind of rough. I cut up an old rubber glove for a skid pad, and tied it onto the bottom with monofilament fishing line. Then I made a knee cushion on top with leather and foam rubber, and with a belt hooked up a strap that Randy could tighten around his thigh to hold the thing in place. One afternoon on the boat I bent my leg at the knee and gave it a try. It was wobbly, but it worked. You could get used to it.

After we'd cruised on out beyond the lighthouse, I brought the stick-leg out and showed it to Randy. He studied it a minute, then threw it across the aisle to the bunk and hopped out into the sunlight to sit on the fish box.

Dad shook his head, his eyes on the water.

I decided to go up on the roof for some fresh air.

At about ten o'clock the boat rolled suddenly into a starboard turn. It took only a few seconds to find what Dad had seen.

Noio.

Seabirds, hundreds of agitated terns working about three acres of ocean, the mass of them rising against the pale blue outline of Mauna Loa in the far distance, then one after another falling and slapping the water to lure the fish up. Would Randy shoot at them? If he did he wouldn't be shooting long with Dad around.

I scrambled down from the roof.

Dad edged the frothing ocean where zillions of flying fish skimmed the water, trying to escape larger fish below and birds above. I grabbed one of the big reels and started pulling in the lure.

"Never mind those," Dad called. "Randy and I

will get them. You get a small rig ready for catching a bait fish."

He throttled down to neutral and ran back to the reels. "Randy, bring in the line on the starboard outrigger. I'll get this one."

I plowed through a box of lures in a drawer under the bunk. "Get a pink one," Dad called over his shoulder. "They'll strike pink before anything else. Pink with a pearl head. Randy!"

Randy didn't move.

I grabbed the lure he wanted and attached it directly onto a fifteen-pound-test nylon line, skipping the more visible wire leader. Dad told us long ago that fish had brains, good ones, and could spot a fake a mile away.

Dad reeled in both big rigs and carried them into the cabin. He laid them on the bunk, ignoring Randy as he passed.

Randy stared at some spot on the sea, somewhere far away.

Dad brought the boat back up to trolling speed.

I set the bait rig in a rod socket and dropped the pink lure into the wake, letting out about seventy-five yards of line.

"Set the drag loose so it won't beat up the fish," Dad shouted from the wheel. "When it comes, it's going to come fast. I can feel it."

We wove in and out of the feeding birds, dragging the single pearl-headed lure, moving in the same direction as the running fish.

A couple of years ago Randy would have been pacing the deck, throwing out his own ideas, and Dad would have saluted and said, "Yessir, cap'm sir, so solly, cap'm."

When the reel started clicking, hooking a small bait fish, Dad throttled down, put the boat in neutral. I reeled the fish in, slow and easy, so I wouldn't damage it.

Randy sat, looking bored.

Dad came back with a heavy trolling rig and a threaded twelve-inch bait needle. He set the rod in a holder, then bent over the transom and lifted the small, striped fish aboard. A kawakawa, maybe eight pounds.

Dad turned it upside down, covering its eyes with his hand to calm it. When the fish was still, Dad held it belly-up in the palm of his hand. It didn't twitch a muscle. It was as if it had been hypnotized.

Randy watched Dad work but smirked when I caught him looking.

Dad removed the lure and threaded the bait needle through the kawakawa's eye sockets, just above the eyeballs, right eye to left, and made a loop. Then he ran the large live-bait hook through the loop and twisted it into place. When he was finished, the hook stood point-up on the head of the fish like the comb on the head of a rooster.

The instant he finished, Dad leaned out over the transom and put the fish back into the ocean. It swam off, sluggish at first, but soon burst down into the depths.

All of it took less than twenty seconds.

I peered over the gunnel and watched the fish dive. Flickering silver flashes of sunlight glinted off its flanks and shot back up from the deep, royal blue water.

"We'll let him run a bit," Dad said, setting the reel on free spool. "Gotta look natural."

Exhaust sputtered out from under the hull whenever the stern rose out of the water. I dug into the cooler for a Coke and tossed one over to Randy. He must have been pretty hot, wearing jeans the way he did to cover up his leg. He put the bottle up against his forehead.

Dad held the line and let it run through his fingers, feeling every move the fish made in his fingertips. "He's scared. Going deep."

When the bait fish stopped its dive, Dad told me to bring the boat up a notch. I went forward and inched the throttle to a crawl.

Looking back through the cabin, I saw Randy's head in shadowy silhouette, and beyond, Dad worked the fish in brilliant, open-deck sunlight.

Still holding on to the line, Dad glanced over his shoulder at Randy. "You ready for some fishing, son?"

"You catch 'um," Randy said.

"Can't. Got to gaff it and bring it aboard."

"Then Jake."

Dad shook his head. "Listen. Plenty guys have

problems worse than yours. You want to lie around and feel sorry for yourself, well, that's your decision. But think about this, is that how you want to live your life from now on?"

Randy turned away.

The boat inched forward, rocking hypnotically in the swells as we trolled through the birds.

"He's running," Dad said suddenly. "Jake, come."

I put the boat on auto pilot and ran aft. The line tightened in Dad's hand and moved off to the port side of the boat.

"He's spooked."

Dad dropped the line. "Take it," he whispered out into the ocean. "Go on, now."

The reel clicked, then stopped, and clicked again.

Dad ran into the cabin to the controls, but before he got there, the reel burst awake, screaming as line raced off, bending the rod nearly to the water.

Dad jammed the boat full throttle, just for a second, then brought her down.

I unhooked the safety line but left the rod in place and looked back into the cabin.

"Randy," Dad shouted. "This one's yours."

Randy almost spat when he answered, "I told you I'm *out* of it!" He grabbed his rifle and pumped a bullet into the chamber, then fired out to sea.

The reel screamed, the fish running, running.

Dad looked as if he were ready to wring Randy's neck. "You take it, Jake," he said, still glaring at Randy.

I yanked the rod from the socket and jerked back on it twice, striking the fish one last time. Line burned off the reel as I braced against the pull, trying to release the drag and ease the pressure. I worked it back to the fighting chair and placed the butt of the rod into the silvery socket and put my feet on the foot brace.

Line whipped back and forth off the spool, tearing out into the ocean.

"Let him go a minute," Dad said, running out. "When he slows, tighten up on the drag and hold him."

The line emptied off the reel so fast I thought there'd be nothing left but a clean spool. The fish managed to rip off five or six hundred yards before I could slowly tighten the drag and choke off the run.

Dad ran back to the wheel and pushed the throttle forward, pulling the boat away from the approaching line. A moment later he let the boat rock in neutral, waiting at the controls.

"I think you got yourself a tuna, Jake."

The birds moved off a hundred yards or so, now scattered. The weight on the line was so intense I had to hold my breath when I pulled back, teeth jammed, my face ready to explode.

I'd almost forgotten about Randy, thinking only of the fish, when he startled me, suddenly at the transom dipping a bucket into the ocean, one of his crutches lying on the floorboards.

He set the bucket on deck. "You think you can handle this, little man?"

"Pshh. In my sleep," I said.

He grunted, then hobbled away.

He returned a minute later with a fat natural sponge, which he soaked in the bucket, then squeezed over my head. It chilled at first but ran soothingly down my neck. "Use your legs," he said. "It's all in the legs."

I studied the water. The fish wasn't running but was still pulling away from me with more muscle than I could return.

I pulled back on the rod until the tendons in my neck ached.

Time passed.

An hour, maybe more.

Dad wandered out every now and then, but mostly he stayed at the wheel.

Randy dragged himself off the fish box to drip another sponge of water down my neck, then on the reel.

"Thanks, bro."

"Running out of gas?"

"Never."

Randy patted me on the back, like he would a child. "Just don't pop a gut, ah?"

Once, the fish made a run, and Dad backed the boat down after it. I reeled in the slack, a few inches. Then the fish stopped and held.

I'd been struggling with it since noon, when the sun was high and the water reflected the cloudless, blue sky. I wondered if I'd end up with only the head, like old Steve from before. But there were no jerks on the line, which was a good sign.

By four-thirty everything had turned gray, and the surface chop had grown restless.

And so had Dad.

"Cut the line, already," he finally called from the cabin. I couldn't see him, but I imagined him sitting at the table with a beer, playing solitaire and shaking his head every time a card stumped him.

"No," I said.

Randy snickered.

Dad came out on the deck and stood beside me. "You got a dead fish. You got a thousand pounds of pressure. Cut it. Let's go home."

Dad opened up his pocketknife. "Come on, Jake. You don't have the juice."

He reached for the line.

"I can do it! Look at the reel, I'm gaining."

"Sorry, Jake," Dad said, bringing the knife up.

Randy's crutch suddenly appeared between the knife and the line. "Time to let a real man do the work."

Still holding the knife near the tip of the rod, Dad cocked his head toward me. "Did you hear something? I thought there were only two fisher-men aboard this boat."

Randy pushed Dad's shoulder with his crutch. "Step aside, gramps."

Then he turned to me. "Let me show you how it's done, son."

"But I've almost got it."

"Nothing is what you got."

I took a deep breath, then leaned forward and let Dad unhitch the harness from the reel. He winked at me, and I got it. Dad wouldn't cut a line in a million years. I don't know why that hadn't clicked in my brain when he'd brought out the knife.

I stepped out of the fighting chair as Randy took hold of the rod. "I guess it won't hurt to let you clean up," I said.

Randy threw his crutch over to the fish box and slipped in around the rod. Dad hooked the harness around Randy's back. For all our joking, reeling in a dead fish, if it was dead, was nothing but pure hard work.

Randy started to pull but had a difficult time balancing his weight on one foot. He gave us a sampling of some of the words he'd learned in the army, then finally gave in. "All right, get me that stupid stick you made and strap it on."

Dad raised his eyebrows.

I went in and got the stick-leg off the bunk. The strapping part was kind of awkward, but it held the contraption in place well enough. Randy lifted it and tapped the rubber end on the foot brace. "Too long," he said, but went on working the fish anyway.

He sank his teeth into the job like a dog on a pig, taking back a good hundred yards of line before stopping to rest.

An hour later all the line was back on the reel. Not bad, I had to admit.

Dad and I stood peering into the water for the first glimpse of whatever it was.

Dad stood back and gave Randy a pat on the back. "Keep her steady, Long John. You've almost got it beat."

The wire leader came inching out of the water. Randy reeled it all the way to the eye on the tip of the rod. Dad reached out over the transom. Hand over hand, he pulled the mysterious fish the last few feet to the boat.

I got the gaff and stood ready.

Randy unhitched the harness and let it fall to the floorboards but stayed in the fighting chair. He took off the stick-leg and threw it on the deck by the fish box.

I gaffed the fish under the gills. There was no explosion of flapping and splashing as Dad leaned over the transom, strained it up over the gunnel, and let it thud to the deck.

"Son of a gun," he said.

A huge bullet-shaped yellowfin tuna. Dead, but not shark-eaten. The dark blue-black ridge of its back and striking golden fin above shiny silver sides spread back from a huge round eye, thickening out into a fat body.

Dad squatted down for a closer look. "Two hundred fifty pounds, be my guess."

He glanced up at Randy and laughed. Randy wore the face of a man dead beat into the ground.

Bent and bowlegged under the weight, Dad hauled the tuna into the fish box and spread ice over it.

Randy rose up and set the rod into a rod holder. He flicked his eyebrows at me, then put a hand on my shoulder and, leaning on me, hopped back to look in the fish box.

Dad dug us both a Coke out of the cooler and threw over a bag of Saloon Pilot crackers. "Let's go home, boys."

I stowed the fishing rods in the rack above the bunk and sat on the floor beside the table to rewind the loose leaders. The muscles in my forearms were as tight as wet rope.

I glanced back at Randy sitting again on the edge of the fish box, a lone silhouette rising and falling against an empty horizon. He'd only shot the rifle once all day.

Randy reached down to the deck for the stickleg, picked it up, and ran his hand along its length as if removing dust.

I turned to Dad, but he was dozing at the wheel.

When I looked back, Randy was trying to make

the stick-leg stay on, strapping it tighter, then pushing himself up to test it.

I went out and sat on the transom facing him.

Randy took the stick-leg off and threw it to me. "That thing works all right, but it looks like something your dogs gnawed on."

I half-laughed and turned it over in my hands. "It does, doesn't it? I'll make you a better one."

I stood to throw the stick-leg overboard.

"Wait, wait!" Randy shouted. "How you expect me to get off this tub? Gimme that thing."

I gaped back at him.

"Come on," he said.

I lobbed it over.

Randy caught it and set it down on the fish box next to him. "Get me something else to drink, will you, bro? That stinking fish wore me out."

The lush green island bobbed ahead as we droned closer to the harbor. I stood on the bow with rope in my hands and my mind at peace. I knew now that when it was my turn to creep through those deadly jungles, I'd think back to Randy and that ridiculous-looking stick-leg, and I'd remember how brave he was, stubborning it out to make that ugly thing work just because I'd made it for him.

That would help. That would help me fight my fear. And if I had to limp home, too, I knew he'd be there to help me keep on going.

And that was enough.

about the author

Graham Salisbury's family has lived in the Hawaiian Islands since the early 1800s. He grew up on Oahu and on Hawaii and graduated from California State University. He earned an M.F.A. from Vermont College of Norwich University, where he was a member of the founding faculty of the M.F.A. program in writing for children. He lives with his family in Portland, Oregon.

His first novel, *Blue Skin of the Sea,* won the Bank Street Child Study Association Children's Book Award, the Judy Lopez Award, and the Oregon Book Award and was selected as an ALA Best Book for Young Adults. *Under the Blood-Red Sun* won the Scott O'Dell Award for Historical Fiction, the Oregon Book Award, Hawaii's Nene Award, and the California Young Reader Medal, was an ALA Notable Book and Best Book for Young

Adults, and is on many state award lists. *Shark Bait* was selected for the Oregon Book Award and as a *Parents' Choice* Silver Honor Book, and *Jungle Dogs* was an ALA Best Book for Young Adults. His most recent novel was *Lord of the Deep*.

Graham Salisbury has been a recipient of the John Unterecker Award for Fiction and the PEN/Norma Klein Award.

You can visit Graham Salisbury at his Web site: www.grahamsalisbury.com.